The Waxwork & Other Stories by AM Burrage

Alfred McLelland Burrage was born in Hillingdon, Middlesex on 1st July, 1889. His father and uncle were both writers, primarily of boy's fiction, and by age 16 AM Burrage had joined them. The young man had ambitions to write for the adult market too. The money was better and so was his writing.

From 1890 to 1914, prior to the mainstream appeal of cinema and radio the printed word, mainly in magazines, was the foremost mass entertainment. AM Burrage quickly became a master of the market publishing his stories regularly across a number of publications.

By the start of the Great War Burrage was well established but in 1916 he was conscripted to fight on the Western Front. He continued to write during these years documenting his experiences in the classic book War is War by Ex-Private X.

For the remainder of his life Burrage was rarely printed in book form but continued to write and be published on a prodigious scale in magazines and newspapers. In this volume we concentrate on his supernatural stories which are, by common consent, some of the best ever written. Succinct yet full of character each reveals a twist and a flavour that is unsettling.....sometimes menacing....always disturbing.

There are many other volumes available in this series together with a number of audiobooks. All are available from iTunes, Amazon and other fine digital stores.

Table Of Contents
The Waxwork
The Case of Mr Ryalstone
One Who Saw
The Running Tide
The Oak Saplings
The Blue Bonnet
Through The Eyes Of A Child
Mr. Garshaw's Companion
The Cottage In The Wood
The Strange Case of Dolly Frewan
The Sweeper
AM Burrage – The Life And Times

The Waxwork

While the uniformed attendants of Marriner's Waxworks were ushering the last stragglers through the great glass-panelled double doors, the manager sat in his office interviewing Raymond Hewson.

The manager was a youngish man, stout, blond and of medium height. He wore his clothes well and contrived to look extremely smart without appearing over-dressed. Raymond Hewson looked neither. His clothes, which had been good when new and which were still carefully brushed and pressed, were beginning to show signs of their owner's losing battle with the world.

He was a small, spare, pale man, with lank, errant brown hair, and although he spoke plausibly and even forcibly he had the defensive and somewhat furtive air of a man who was used to rebuffs. He looked what he was, a man gifted somewhat above the ordinary, who was a failure through his lack of self-assertion.

The manager was speaking.

'There is nothing new in your request,' he said, in fact we refuse it to different people—mostly young bloods who have tried to make bets—about three times a week. We have nothing to gain and something to lose by letting people spend the night in our Murderers' Den. If I allowed it, and some young idiot lost his senses, what would be my position? But your being a journalist somewhat alters the case.'

Hewson smiled.

'I suppose you mean that journalists have no senses to lose.'

'No, no,' laughed the manager, 'but one imagines them to be responsible people. Besides, here we have something to gain; publicity and advertisement.'

'Exactly,' said Hewson, 'and there I thought we might come to terms.'

The manager laughed again.

'Oh,' he exclaimed, 'I know what's coming. You want to be paid twice, do you? It used to be said years ago that Madame Tussaud's would give a man a hundred pounds for sleeping alone in the Chamber of Horrors. I hope you don't think that we have made any such offer. Er—what is your paper, Mr Hewson?'

'I am freelancing at present,' Hewson confessed, 'working on space for several papers. However, I should find no difficulty in getting the story printed. The Morning Echo would use it like a shot. "A Night with Marriner's Murderers". No live paper could turn it down.'

The manager rubbed his chin.

'Ah! And how do you propose to treat it?'

'I shall make it gruesome, of course; gruesome with just a saving touch of humour.'

The other nodded and offered Hewson his cigarette-case.

'Very well, Mr Hewson,' he said. 'Get your story printed in the Morning Echo, and there will be a five-pound note waiting for you here when you care to come and call for it. But first of all, it's no small ordeal that you're proposing to undertake. I'd like to be quite sure about you, and I'd like you to be quite sure about yourself. I own I shouldn't care to take it on. I've seen those figures dressed and undressed, I know all about the process of their manufacture, I can walk about in company downstairs as unmoved as if I were walking among so many skittles, but I should hate having to sleep down there alone among them.'

'Why?' asked Hewson.

'I don't know. There isn't any reason. I don't believe in ghosts. If I did I should expect them to haunt the scene of their crimes or the spot where their bodies were laid, instead of a cellar which happens to contain their waxwork effigies. It's just that I couldn't sit alone among them all night, with their seeming to stare at me in the way they do. After all, they represent the lowest and most appalling types of humanity, and—although I would not own it publicly—the people who come to see them are not generally charged with the very highest motives. The whole atmosphere of the place is unpleasant, and if you are susceptible to atmosphere I warn you that you are in for a very uncomfortable night.'

Hewson had known that from the moment when the idea had first occurred to him. His soul sickened at the prospect, even while he smiled casually upon the manager. But he had a wife and family to keep, and for the past month he had been living on paragraphs, eked out by his rapidly dwindling store of savings. Here was a chance not to be missed—the price of a special story in the Morning Echo, with a five-pound note to add to it. It meant comparative wealth and luxury for a week, and freedom from the worst anxieties for a fortnight. Besides, if he wrote the story well, it might lead to an offer of regular employment.

'The way of transgressors—and newspaper men—is hard,' he said, 'I have already promised myself an uncomfortable night, because your murderers' den is obviously not fitted up as an hotel bedroom. But I don't think your waxworks will worry me much.'

'You're not superstitious?'

'Not a bit.' Hewson laughed.

'But you're a journalist; you must have a strong imagination.'

'The news editors for whom I've worked have always complained that I haven't any. Plain facts are not considered sufficient in our trade, and the papers don't like offering their readers unbuttered bread.'

The manager smiled and rose.

'Right,' he said, i think the last of the people have gone. Wait a moment. I'll give orders for the figures downstairs not to be draped, and let the night people know that you'll be here. Then I'll take you down and show you round.'

He picked up the receiver of a house telephone, spoke into it and presently replaced it.

'One condition I'm afraid I must impose on you,' he remarked, 'I must ask you not to smoke. We had a fire scare down in the Murderers' Den this evening. I don't know who gave the alarm, but whoever it was it was a false one. Fortunately there were very few people down there at the time, or there might have been a panic. And now, if you're ready, we'll make a move.'

Hewson followed the manager through half a dozen rooms where attendants were busy shrouding the kings and queens of England, the generals and prominent statesmen of this and other generations, all the mixed herd of humanity whose fame or notoriety had rendered them eligible for this kind of immortality. The manager stopped once and spoke to a man in uniform, saying something about an arm-chair in the Murderers' Den.

'It's the best we can do for you, I'm afraid,' he said to Hewson. 'I hope you'll be able to get some sleep.'

He led the way through an open barrier and down ill-lit stone stairs which conveyed a sinister impression of giving access to a dungeon. In a passage at the bottom were a few preliminary horrors, such as relics of the Inquisition, a rack taken from a mediaeval castle, branding irons, thumbscrews, and other mementoes of man's one-time cruelty to man. Beyond the passage was the Murderers' Den.

It was a room of irregular shape with a vaulted roof, and dimly lit by electric lights burning behind inverted bowls of frosted glass. It was, by design, an eerie and uncomfortable chamber—a chamber whose atmosphere invited its visitors to speak in whispers. There was something of the air of a chapel about it, but a chapel no longer devoted to the practice of piety and given over now for base and impious worship.

The waxwork murderers stood on low pedestals with numbered tickets at their feet. Seeing them elsewhere, and without knowing whom they represented, one would have thought them a dull-looking crew, chiefly remarkable for the shabbiness of their clothes, and as evidence of the changes of fashion even among the unfashionable.

Recent notorieties rubbed dusty shoulders with the old 'favourites'. Thurtell, the murderer of Weir, stood as if frozen in the act of making a shop-window gesture to young Bywaters. There was Lefroy, the poor half-baked little snob who killed for gain so that he might ape the gentleman.   Within five yards of him sat Mrs Thompson, that erotic romanticist, hanged to propitiate British middle-class matronhood. Charles Peace, the only member of that vile company who looked uncompromisingly and entirely evil, sneered across a gangway at Norman Thorne. Browne and Kennedy, the two most recent additions, stood between Mrs Dyer and Patrick Mahon. The manager, walking around with Hewson, pointed out several of the more interesting of these unholy notabilities.

'That's Crippen; I expect you recognize him. Insignificant little beast who looks as if he couldn't tread on a worm. That's Armstrong. Looks like a decent, harmless country gentleman, doesn't he? There's old Vaquier; you can't miss him because of his beard. And of course this'

'Who's that?' Hewson interrupted in a whisper, pointing.

'Oh, I was coming to him,' said the manager in a light undertone. 'Come and have a good look at him. This is our star turn. He's the only one of the bunch that hasn't been hanged.'

The figure which Hewson had indicated was that of a small, slight man not much more than five feet in height. It wore little waxed moustaches, large spectacles, and a caped coat. There was something so exaggeratedly French in its appearance that it reminded Hewson of a stage caricature. He could not have said precisely why the mild-looking face seemed to him so repellent, but he had already recoiled a step and, even in the manager's company, it cost him an effort to look again.

'But who is he?' he asked.

'That,' said the manager, 'is Dr Bourdette.'

Hewson shook his head doubtfully.

'I think I've heard the name,' he said, 'but I forget in connection with what. '

The manager smiled.

'You'd remember better if you were a Frenchman,' he said. 'For some long while that man was the terror of Paris. He carried on his work of healing by day, and of throat-cutting by night, when the fit was on him. He killed for the sheer devilish pleasure it gave him to kill, and always in the same way—with a razor. After his last crime he left a clue behind him which set the police upon his track. One clue led to another, and before very long they knew that they were on the track of the Parisian equivalent of our Jack the Ripper, and had enough evidence to send him to the madhouse or the guillotine on a dozen capital charges.

'But even then our friend here was too clever for them. When he realized that the toils were closing about him he mysteriously disappeared, and ever since the police of every civilized country have been looking for him. There is no doubt that he managed to make away with himself, and by some means which has prevented his body coming to light. One or two crimes of a similar nature have taken place since his disappearance, but he is believed almost for certain to be dead, and the experts believe these recrudescences to be the work of an imitator. It's queer, isn't it, how every notorious murderer has imitators?'

Hewson shuddered and fidgeted with his feet.

'I don't like him at all,' he confessed. 'Ugh! What eyes he's got!'

'Yes, this figure's a little masterpiece. You find the eyes bite into you?

Well, that's excellent realism, then, for Bourdette practised mesmerism, and was supposed to mesmerize his victims before dispatching them. Indeed, had he not done so, it is impossible to see how so small a man could have done his ghastly work. There were never any signs of a struggle.'

'I thought I saw him move,' said Hewson with a catch in his voice.

The manager smiled.

'You'll have more than one optical illusion before the night's out, I expect. You shan't be locked in. You can come upstairs when you've had enough of it. There are watchmen on the premises, so you'll find company. Don't be alarmed if you hear them moving about. I'm sorry I can't give you any more light, because all the lights are on. For obvious reasons we keep this place as gloomy as possible. And now I think you had better return with me to the office and have a tot of whisky before beginning your night's vigil.'

The member of the night staff who placed the arm-chair for Hewson was inclined to be facetious.

'Where will you have it, sir?' he asked, grinning. 'Just 'ere, so as you can 'ave a little talk with Crippen when you're tired of sitting still? Or there's old Mother Dyer over there, making eyes and looking as if she could do with a bit of company. Say where, sir.'

Hewson smiled. The man's chaff pleased him if only because, for the moment at least, it lent the proceedings a much-desired air of the commonplace.

'I'll place it myself, thanks,' he said, 'I'll find out where the draughts come from first.'

'You won't find any down here. Well, good night, sir. I'm upstairs if you want me. Don't let 'em sneak up behind you and touch your neck with their cold and clammy 'ands. And you look out for that old Mrs Dyer; I believe she's taken a fancy to you.'

Hewson laughed and wished the man good night. It was easier than he had expected. He wheeled the arm-chair—a heavy one upholstered in plush—a little way down the central gangway, and deliberately turned it so that its back was towards the effigy of Dr Bourdette. For some undefined reason he liked Dr Bourdette a great deal less than his companions.

Busying himself with arranging the chair he was almost light-hearted, but when the attendant's footfalls had died away and a deep hush stole over the chamber he realized that he had no slight ordeal before him.   The dim unwavering light fell on the rows of figures which were so uncannily like human beings that the silence and the stillness seemed unnatural and even ghastly. He missed the sound of breathing, the rustling of clothes, the hundred and one minute noises one hears when even the deepest silence has fallen upon a crowd. But the air was as stagnant as water at the bottom of a standing pond. There was not a breath in the chamber to stir a curtain or rustle a hanging drapery or start a shadow. His own shadow, moving in response to a shifted arm or leg, was all that could be coaxed into motion. All was still to the gaze and silent to the ear. it must be like this at the bottom of the sea,' he thought, and wondered how to work the phrase into his story on the morrow.

He faced the sinister figures boldly enough. They were only waxworks.

So long as he let that thought dominate all others he promised himself that all would be well. It did not, however, save him long from the discomfort occasioned by the waxen stare of Dr Bourdette, which, he knew, was directed upon him from behind. The eyes of the little Frenchman's effigy haunted and tormented him, and he itched with the desire to turn and look.

'Come!' he thought, 'my nerves have started already. If I turn and look at that dressed-up dummy it will be an admission of funk.'

And then another voice in his brain spoke to him.

'It's because you're afraid that you won't turn and look at him.'

The two Voices quarrelled silently for a moment or two, and at last Hewson slewed his chair round a little and looked behind him.

Among the many figures standing in stiff, unnatural poses, the effigy of the dreadful little doctor stood out with a queer prominence, perhaps because a steady beam of light beat straight down upon it. Hewson flinched before the parody of mildness which some fiendishly skilled craftsman had managed to convey in wax, met the eyes for one agonized second, and turned again to face the other direction.

'He's only a waxwork like the rest of you,' Hewson muttered defiantly.

'You're all only waxworks.'

They were only waxworks, yes, but waxworks don't move. Not that he had seen the least movement anywhere, but it struck him that, in the moment or two while he had looked behind him, there had been the least subtle change in the grouping of the figures in front. Crippen, for instance, seemed to have turned at least one degree to the left. Or, thought Hewson, perhaps the illusion was due to the fact that he had not slewed his chair back into its exact original position. And there were Field and Grey, too; surely one of them had moved his hands. Hewson held his breath for a moment, and then drew his courage back to him as a man lifts a weight. He remembered the words of more than one news editor and laughed savagely to himself. 'And they tell me I've got no imagination!' he said beneath his breath.

He took a notebook from his pocket and wrote quickly.

'Mem.—Deathly silence and unearthly stillness of figures. Like being bottom of sea. Hypnotic eyes of Dr Bourdette. Figures seem to move when not being watched.'

He closed the book suddenly over his fingers and looked round quickly and awfully over his right shoulder. He had neither seen nor heard a movement, but it was as if some sixth sense had made him aware of one. He looked straight into the vapid countenance of Lefroy which smiled vacantly back as if to say, it wasn't I!'

Of course it wasn't he, or any of them; it was his own nerves. Or was it?

Hadn't Crippen moved again during that moment when his attention was directed elsewhere. You couldn't trust that little man! Once you took your eyes off him he took advantage of it to shift his position. That was what they were all doing, if he only knew it, he told himself; and half-rose out of his chair. This was not quite good enough! He was going. He wasn't going to spend the night with a lot of waxworks which moved while he wasn't looking.

. . . Hewson sat down again. This was very cowardly and very absurd. They were only waxworks and they couldn't move; let him hold that thought and all would yet be well. Then why all that silent unrest about him?—a subtle something in the air which did not quite break the silence and happened, whichever way he looked, just beyond the boundaries of his vision.

He swung round quickly to encounter the mild but baleful stare of Dr Bourdette. Then, without warning, he jerked his head back to stare straight at Crippen. Ha! he'd nearly caught Crippen that time!

'You'd better be careful, Crippen—and all the rest of you! If I do see one of you move I'll smash you to pieces! Do you hear?'

He ought to go, he told himself. Already he had experienced enough to write his story, or ten stories for the matter of that. Well, then, why not go? The Morning Echo would be none the wiser as to how long he had stayed, nor would it care so long as his story was a good one. Yes, but that night watchman upstairs would chaff him. And the manager—one never knew—perhaps the manager would quibble over that five-pound note which he needed so badly. He wondered if Rose were asleep or if she were lying awake and thinking of him. She'd laugh when he told her that he had imagined . . .

This was a little too much! It was bad enough that the waxwork effigies of murderers should move when they weren't being watched, but it was intolerable that they should breathe. Somebody was breathing. Or was it his own breath which sounded to him as if it came from a distance? He sat rigid, listening and straining, until he exhaled with a long sigh. His own breath after all, or—if not, Something had divined that he was listening and had ceased breathing simultaneously.

Hewson jerked his head swiftly around and looked all about him out of haggard and haunted eyes. Everywhere his gaze encountered the vacant waxen faces, and everywhere he felt that by just some least fraction of a second had he missed seeing a movement of hand or foot, a silent opening or compression of lips, a flicker of eyelids, a look of human intelligence now smoothed out. They were like naughty children in a class, whispering, fidgeting and laughing behind their teacher's back, but blandly innocent when his gaze was turned upon them.

This would not do! This distinctly would not do! He must clutch at something, grip with his mind upon something which belonged essentially to the workaday world, to the daylight London streets. He was Raymond Hewson, an unsuccessful journalist, a living and breathing man, and these figures grouped around him were only dummies, so they could neither move nor whisper. What did it matter if they were supposed to be lifelike effigies of murderers? They were only made of wax and sawdust, and stood there for the entertainment of morbid sightseers and orange-sucking trippers. That was better! Now what was that funny story which somebody had told him in the Fal staff yesterday? . . .

He recalled part of it, but not all, for the gaze of Dr Bourdette urged, challenged, and finally compelled him to turn.

Hewson half-turned, and then swung his chair so as to bring him face to face with the wearer of those dreadful hypnotic eyes. His own eyes were dilated, and his mouth, at first set in a grin of terror, lifted at the corners in a snarl. Then Hewson spoke and woke a hundred sinister echoes.

'You moved, damn you!' he cried. 'Yes, you did, damn you! I saw you!'

Then he sat quite still, staring straight before him like a man found frozen in the Arctic snows.

Dr Bourdette's movements were leisurely. He stepped off his pedestal with the mincing care of a lady alighting from a 'bus. The platform stood about two feet from the ground, and above the edge of it a plush-covered rope hung in arc-like curves. Dr Bourdette lifted up the rope until it formed an arch for him to pass under, stepped off the platform and sat down on the edge, facing Hewson. Then he nodded and smiled and said 'Good evening. I need hardly tell you,' he continued, in perfect English in which was traceable only the least foreign accent, 'that not until I overheard the conversation between you and the worthy manager of this establishment, did I suspect that I should have the pleasure of a companion here for the night. You cannot move or speak without my bidding, but you can hear me perfectly well. Something tells me that you are—shall I say nervous? My dear sir, have no illusions. I am not one of these contemptible effigies miraculously come to life; I am Dr Bourdette himself.'

He paused, coughed and shifted his legs.

'Pardon me,' he resumed, 'but I am a little stiff. And let me explain. Circumstances with which I need not fatigue you, have made it desirable that I should live in England. I was close to this building this evening when I saw a policeman regarding me a thought too curiously. I guessed that he intended to follow and perhaps ask me embarrassing questions, so I mingled with the crowd and came in here. An extra coin bought my admission to the chamber in which we now meet, and an inspiration showed me a certain means of escape.

'I raised a cry of fire, and when all the fools had rushed to the stairs I stripped my effigy of the caped coat which you behold me wearing, donned it, hid my effigy under the platform at the back, and took its place on the pedestal.

'I own that I have since spent a very fatiguing evening, but fortunately I was not always being watched and had opportunities to draw an occasional deep breath and ease the rigidity of my pose. One small boy screamed and exclaimed that he saw me moving. I understood that he was to be whipped and put straight to bed on his return home, and I can only hope that the threat has been executed to the letter.

'The manager's description of me, which I had the embarrassment of being compelled to overhear, was biased but not altogether inaccurate. Clearly I am not dead, although it is as well that the world thinks otherwise. His account of my hobby, which I have indulged for years, although, through necessity, less frequently of late, was in the main true although not intelligently expressed. The world is divided between collectors and non-collectors. With the non-collectors we are not concerned. The collectors collect anything, according to their individual tastes, from money to cigarette cards, from moths to matchboxes. I collect throats.'

He paused again and regarded Hewson's throat with interest mingled with disfavour.

'I am obliged to the chance which brought us together to-night,' he continued, 'and perhaps it would seem ungrateful to complain. From motives of personal safety my activities have been somewhat curtailed of late years, and I am glad of this opportunity of gratifying my somewhat unusual whim. But you have a skinny neck, sir, if you will overlook a personal remark. I should never have selected you from choice. I like men with thick necks . . . thick red necks . . .'

He fumbled in an inside pocket and took out something which he tested against a wet forefinger and then proceeded to pass gently to and fro across the palm of his left hand.

'This is a little French razor,' he remarked blandly. 'They are not much used in England, but perhaps you know them? One strops them on wood. The blade, you will observe, is very narrow. They do not cut very deep, but deep enough. In just one little moment you shall see for yourself. I shall ask you the little civil question of all the polite barbers: Does the razor suit you, sir?' He rose up, a diminutive but menacing figure of evil, and approached Hewson with the silent, furtive step of a hunting panther.

'You will have the goodness,' he said, 'to raise your chin a little. Thank you, and a little more. Just a little more. Ah, thank you! . . . Merci, m'sieur . . . Ah, merci. . . merci. . .'

Over one end of the chamber was a thick skylight of frosted glass which, by day, let in a few sickly and filtered rays from the floor above. After sunrise these began to mingle with the subdued light from the electric bulbs, and this mingled illumination added a certain ghastliness to a scene which needed no additional touch of horror.

The waxwork figures stood apathetically in their places, waiting to be admired or execrated by the crowds who would presently wander fearfully among them. In their midst, in the centre gangway, Hewson sat still, leaning far back in his arm-chair. His chin was uptilted as if he were waiting to receive attention from a barber, and although there was not a scratch upon his throat, nor anywhere upon his body, he was cold and dead. His previous employers were wrong in having credited him with no imagination.

Dr Bourdette on his pedestal watched the dead man unemotionally. He did not move, nor was he capable of motion. But then, after all, he was only a waxwork.

The Case of Mr Ryalstone

I was aware of having seen him once or twice before, but I did not know his name. He was short and grey and elderly and looked rather mouse-like in his dark worsted lounge suit. There was nothing attractive nor repellent in his round pale face; indeed he seemed to me almost entirely lacking in personality.

It was a dark dismal Sunday afternoon with a mist of rain on the Club windows. Outside a mortuary there is nothing drearier nor more deserted than a London club on a wet Sunday afternoon. We were the only two in the great smoking-room and shared the hearth, sitting one on either side. I had taken possession of a pile of Sunday papers and, having skimmed their contents, was dropping them one by one beside my chair. My companion was reading a novel from the Club library—or rather skipping it, for I heard him flick over bunches of the leaves with his thumb, as one shuffling a pack of cards.

I suppose I wore an air of somnolence similar to his. The quietness about us, the heat of the fire, and the general atmosphere of Sunday afternoon with its attendant boredom, were all conducive to drowsiness. By nature I am a gregarious animal and I would have been glad to risk an experiment in conversation. But there was the chance that my vis-a-vis might be one of those absurdly 'sticky' individuals who resent the conversational overtures of strangers, even when those strangers happen to be fellow clubmen. His dimness of personality and—it seemed to me then—the unlikelihood of our being able to find common ground, held me silent. With some men I might have considered it worthwhile to risk a snub, but not with him.

Presently I heard him lay aside his book on the little round table at his elbow, and within a minute or two I had dropped the last of the Sunday papers on the pile beside my chair.

I looked at him as I leaned back. He was right in my line of vision and I could not help gazing at him without moving my chair or slewing my head to an uncomfortable angle. He too was leaning back, and watching me out of half-closed eyes. And suddenly something in the man's expression made me aware that he wanted to talk and had been casting about in his mind for some way of breaking the ice. So I straightened myself a little in my chair and remarked that it was a rotten day.

He smiled then, as if the pestilent weather were something to smile about, and agreed with me.

'The man,' he added in a thin penetrating voice, 'who can devise some means of amusement on a wet Sunday afternoon in London ought to be given a state pension. This evening I shall go to Queen's Hall. Just now I am merely watching the clock and wondering how soon I can honestly tell myself that it's teatime.'

'You staying here?' I asked.

He nodded.

'Yes, I always do when I come up.'

'So do I,' I remarked. 'It's about as comfortable as any place I know. But it's like anywhere else on a wet Sunday. There's nothing to do but read.'

He picked up the book he had been glancing through and held it so that I could read its title.

'You know this, of course?' he asked.

I nodded and smiled. It was Stevenson's Dr Jekyll and Mr Hyde.

'I've read it at least half a dozen times before,' he continued, 'and I've a particular reason for being interested in it. Of course, dual personality is a well-known scientific phenomenon. You believe it possible, I suppose?'

I answered that I supposed I did, and added:

'Of course, the man's body changing with his personality is an attractive piece of romanticism, but it puts the story right outside the pale of the probabilities. The whole thing is allegorical.'

He let his head sink a little as a sign of assent.

'Of course, of course. And yet mind controls matter and even shapes it. You can often tell a man's mental capacity, and even his profession, by his outward appearance. And our scientists are only just beginning to understand the human mind. Fifty years ago a case of dual personality would have been lodged in the nearest mad-house. But while denying the literal possibility of Dr Jekyll changing physically as well as mentally into Mr Hyde, and back into Dr Jekyll again, it begs a question which I should like to ask of somebody who understands these things.'

'I don't,' I said smiling, 'but I should like to hear the question.'

He edged his chair nearer to mine, leaned forward, and spoke very earnestly.

'Would you consider it possible,' he asked, 'for two men, strangers who have never met, leading separate and concurrent existences, to have personalities so interwoven that they are in effect one and the same man. What I am trying to convey is just the opposite to the idea of a dual personality. If two separate beings can dwell consecutively in the one man, is it possible for two men to share the same personality?'

I laughed gently and remarked that it was a good conundrum. He smiled, but only faintly.

'I could tel' you,' he said, 'why that question has been vexing me for some time. The truth is that I am very seriously worried. I don't know if you would care to hear? I think I can promise not to bore you. You will probably think that I am mad, and if you suspect me of purposely romancing you will be paying me a sort of compliment, for I have never in my life been credited with an imagination. For a long while I have been yearning to tell somebody and haven't dared; and just now some instinct assured me that you would be a sympathetic listener.'

'I think I can at least promise to be that,' I assured him.

There was a pause. The small, grey-haired man sat looking into the fire, as if seeking there the inspiration to begin his story.

'You don't know me,' he said at last. 'My name's Ryalstone. I am afraid I shall have to begin by telling you a few details about myself, but I will make them as brief as possible. I am now sixty-two years old. My father was the senior partner of the firm of solicitors in which I joined him as a young man, and from which I retired five years ago. It was a family business, and I was the fourth generation. I was educated at Marlborough and Jesus, Cambridge. I am a bachelor. It is necessary for me to tell you these things in order that you may understand how little I might be expected to know of the intimate details of the life of a corn-chandler in a small country town.

'Since I came down from Cambridge I have lived all my life in and around London. I have taken holidays, of course, and know the Continent and most parts of my own country with the superficial knowledge of the tourist. But before going further I am willing to swear that I have never been in Somerset in my life, except to pass through it in the train on my way to Devon and Cornwall. There is a town called Corystock in Somerset, and I will swear that I have never visited it in the flesh. I have not even passed through it by train, for it is some miles north of the main line. Will you believe that?'

I inclined my head. I too had never been to Corystock, although I was vaguely aware of a town of that name. Ryalstone watched me thoughtfully for a moment and then proceeded.

'I want to make it quite clear that I have never visited Corystock in the flesh, and that my life has been devoid of anything that could be called romantic. I have always been in easy circumstances. Since I have retired I have been able to give much time to my hobbies—my acquisition of Japanese prints, my modest collection of first editions, my study of economics, and my daily rubbers of bridge. There is a great deal of the recluse in me, and I realise that I am a man who has missed a great deal in life but one who is yet left without any sense of loss. I have loved women sporadically, but no one woman has ever made me want to marry her. I should hate to be burdened with children and the establishment of a married man. I am self-contained and, if you will, selfish.

'All my life I have dreamed while asleep, and my dreams were, I imagine, the kind of nonsensical phantasies common to most men. About once a week, perhaps, I would dream something so absurd or bizarre as to seem worth remembering for an hour or two after I woke. That was until about a year ago. Since then I have dreamed very differently.'

A servant came in to look at the fire, and Ryalstone paused until we were once more left alone together.

'Yes,' he resumed, 'it must have been about a year ago when it began. I woke up one morning, conscious of having had a very long and a particularly vivid dream, of which I was able to remember as many details as if it had been my own waking life of the day before.

'I was a big fat man in my dream, and I was a com-chandler named Surridge. I lived in a town in North Somerset called Corystock. My shop was on a corner of the town square, diagonally opposite to a great church which was called the Minster. I had a lean, iron-grey wife who pretended to pet me in public and tried to bully me in private, and a grown-up daughter named Gladys. Gladys was engaged to marry a commercial traveller named George Thirkhill.

'I can't tell you what I actually dreamed on that first occasion, because I was so completely Ben Surridge—my first name was Ben—and I had all Ben Surridge's memories. I had lost all my own identity, and nothing was strange to me because I was Ben Surridge, and I was a com-chandler living in Corystock, with a shop which looked straight across to the square towers of the Minster.

'That first night I went through an uneventful day of Ben Surridge's life. I served in the shop, assisted by my wife and daughter, until half-past twelve. Then, as my custom seemed to be, I went out to a public house called The Stag and drank two half-pints of beer in the company of the landlord and three or four cronies. I went back to midday dinner, and spent the afternoon in making up accounts. The whole thing, I must tell you, was vivid and natural and ordinary. For the time being I was Ben Surridge, and I knew Ben Surridge's business. Not a vestige of my own personality was left, nor had I the least suspicion—as one sometimes has in dreams—of an overshadowing reality. I quoted prices in answers to half a dozen letters, and sent peremptory notes to two poultry farmers whose accounts were overdue. I took cold supper with my wife and daughter, and then went out again to The Stag. I discussed the affairs of the town with my friends—whom I shall name if you wish—returned home, went to bed, and presently woke up as—myself!

'I remembered the dream all next day because, although it seemed so inconsequent, it was so rational and so vivid. I—moi qui vous parle—knew nothing of the business of a corn merchant except what I had picked up in my dreams. I knew Corystock only by name, and I had never heard of a man named Ben Surridge. Yet I was aware that in my dream I had got right into the skin of this imaginary person, and that his habits, mind and memories were as familiar to me as my own very different habits and mind and memories. It was the kind of dream to linger in one's memory because of its wealth of detail, its lack of extravagant absurdities, its amazing and inexplicable air of reality. The dream haunted me all day, and that night, when I went to bed, I went on dreaming it.'

'The same dream all over again?' I asked.

'Oh, dear no!' He laughed faintly, 'I shouldn't have troubled so much about that. But I "woke up" as Ben Surridge, and the events in my previous dream became as the events of yesterday. I just went on with Ben Surridge's life where it was broken off by his falling asleep and my waking up. It's been going on ever since. I am Ben Surridge the corn-chandler of Corystock directly I fall asleep, and directly he falls asleep I wake up again as myself.

This seems perfectly mad and absurd, but it's the only way I can begin to describe it to you. And don't make any mistake—my dreaming life as Ben Surridge, besides being as realistic, is just as consecutive as my own waking life.

'That second night, directly I began to dream, I was Ben Surridge getting out of bed in the morning, and I picked up the threads of my existence just where they were severed at the end of my last dream. I needn't elaborate. It would take me hours, even perhaps days, to give you all the details of this vivid and realistic dream-life of mine.

'Quite the most extraordinary aspect of the affair is my ability to remember things as Surridge which certainly never happened to me as Ryalstone. As Surridge in my dreams I have my retrospective moments. I remember my father, a small farmer, my going to a local elementary school and thence by easy scholarship to the local grammar school. My first sweetheart, the friends of my younger days, I am able to name them all without the least effort of memory. I know that as Surridge I have only been to London twice in my life, and remember how the traffic bothered me. I can recollect having stolen gingerbread at a country fair, and getting well licked for it. I tell you, my dear sir, it's all something more than merely strange. I, Ryalstone, cease when I sleep and become completely Surridge, living his life in every minute detail, feeling the ordinary human needs for food and drink, satisfying my hunger and thirst, and feeling pain, irritation and annoyance and my moments of contentment and elation.

'As Surridge I am rather popular in the town, and I am proud of being considered rather a character. I pass as a wit—God save the mark!—and wake as myself quivering with irritation at the things I have said as Surridge which have brought a laugh. Oh, I could go on telling you these things for ever, but what in Heaven's name do you think of it all?'

I was unprepared for the question, and I could only laugh weakly, 'I should think,' I remarked, 'that you never know whether you're asleep or awake. How do you know, for instance, that you're not dreaming this very moment? Suppose you're really Surridge who consistently dreams that he's Ryalstone. Of course, I know you're not dreaming now, but how do you know?'

'Because as Surridge in my dream I know I have never even heard of such a person as Ryalstone. When to-night I go on dreaming that I am Surridge I shall remember nothing of all this. And I know that it is only about a year ago that I began to be Surridge in my dreams.'

I lit a cigarette and sat regarding him. Frankly I did not know what to say to the man. I could not believe his extravagant and grotesque story but the most elementary courtesy forbade me to tell him so. He had neither the look nor the mannerisms of the common or garden club liar, and the undernote of distress in his voice was uncommonly well done if it were merely acting.

'Is there such a person as Surridge, a corn-chandler of Corystock?' I asked.

'I don't know.'

'Then why not find out?'

'Because I'm terrified in case there should be. Suppose we happened to meet, in God's name what would happen then?'

'It might cause a sort of short circuit,' I suggested. 'You might stop dreaming.'

Ryalstone shifted himself uneasily.

'Yes, I might. But for all I know, life and reason may be at stake. Do you know what I'm beginning to think—to fear?'

I knew instinctively, but he had answered his own question before I could utter the words.

'I believe there is such a man. I believe that when he sleeps to-night he will dream my life of to-day or of to-morrow. If that's so, you see, one of us must always be a little ahead of time. That's a dizzy, shattering, ghastly thought. Only he doesn't remember his dreams, you see. At least, I don't remember them for him when I'm living his life.'

'Have you had—er—medical advice?' I asked awkwardly.

He shook his head vehemently.

'No! What could a doctor say except that I'm off my head? I haven't told a soul except you.'

I inclined my head and greatly wanted to ask him why I had been singled out for the honour of receiving his confidence. But the question must have smacked of sarcasm, and I did not want to wound him. He seemed to read my thoughts, for he said:

'I have very few friends, you see, and I felt that I had to talk to someone to-day.'

'Why to-day?' I asked.

He leaned forward, his fingers twitching nervously.

'Because I'm afraid. Because for the last half dozen nights Surridge has been ill. Last night, in my dream, I was Surridge as usual but I was very weak and hardly conscious. There was a nurse in the room all the time, and my—er—Surridge's wife and daughter had both been crying. A strange man who looked like a doctor came in twice. You know—you must be able to guess—what I've been thinking about all day. Suppose Surridge dies. Suppose'

'You mean,' I amended, 'suppose you dream that he dies?'

'If you like. Well, what then? What's going to happen to me? What'

'Once your subconscious mind had accepted the fact of the man's death, I should think you'd stop dreaming.'

Ryalstone looked at me eagerly and smiled.

'Do you think so?' he asked. 'Do you think it would be only that?'

'What else would you expect?' I queried.

He turned his face from me and looked haggardly into the fire.

'I don't know. I daren't think. God knows I shall be afraid to go to sleep to-night. I shall try hard to keep myself awake. I daren't go on with that dream any longer. Last night was almost too much for me. I was dying and I knew it. Dying's a ghastly sensation. Ghastly!'

It was by now past four o'clock, so we ordered tea and toast, and ate and drank at our ease before the fire. We went on discussing his dreams, but he told me little that was not in the nature of repetition. I still could not bring myself to believe him, but his story had none the less intrigued me, and it had hastened the passing of a dull afternoon.

Presently one of the younger generation looked into the room, pounced on me, and demanded that I should make a fourth at bridge. Ryalstone remarked that it was time he dressed for a very early dinner before leaving for the concert; and so we parted.

At eight o'clock I was back in the smoking-room for a cocktail before dinner, when in stalked Miles Kennedy, whom I hadn't seen for years. He was making that hissing noise of one who grooms horses, and rubbing his flat white hands as if they were frozen.

'You're not cold?' I said, after we had greeted.

'Not cold!' said Kennedy. 'You'd be cold, my lad, if you'd driven up from Somerset to-day. The wind was dead east most of the time. You staying here? What have you been doing with yourself all day?'

'Talking to a man named Ryalstone mostly,' I answered 'Know him?'

Kennedy shook his head.

'Not by name. Who is he?'

'That,' I replied, 'isn't at all an easy question to answer. However, what he told me was confidential so I mustn't pass it on to you. By the way, didn't you say you'd just come up from Somerset?'

'Where the cider apples grow,' said Kennedy, nodding.

'Do you know a town called Corystock?'

'Well, I ought to. My new place is just outside it.'

'You don't happen to know of a corn-dealer named Surridge?'

He laughed reminiscently.

'What, old Ben Surridge! I should think I do! Do you know him, then? He's quite a character. Poor old chap!'

'Why poor old chap?' I asked.

'Because I'm afraid he's going home. Pneumonia, you know. I was in the town last night and heard them talking about him. According to the latest report he hadn't many hours to live.'

'Well, I'm damned!' I exclaimed.

Kennedy eyed me queerly, but I didn't tell him what had wrung the ejaculation from me. An eerie sensation had stolen over me. If Ryalstone had invented his queer story he had certainly spared no pains to make it circumstantial.

I did not see him anymore that night. I heard afterwards that he went straight to his room after returning from Queen's Hall.

The club valet who had charge of my room woke me with early tea at nine on the following morning. I thought that his tread was even softer than usual as he crossed the room to pull up my blind.

'A very sad thing's just happened, sir,' he said, returning to my bedside.

'Did you know Mr Ryalstone?'

I sat up in bed and stared blankly at him.

'Yes,' I began, 'what'

'He was staying here, sir, in Number Eight. I went in with his tea an hour ago and found him lying dead in his bed.'

One Who Saw

There are certain people, often well enough liked, genial souls whom one is always glad to meet, who yet have the faculty of disappearing without being missed. Crutchley must have been one of them. It wasn't until his name was casually mentioned that evening at the Storgates' that most of us remembered that we hadn't seen him about for the last year or two. It was Mrs Storgate's effort at remembering, with the help of those nearest her at table, the guests at a certain birthday party of four years since that was the cause of Crutchley's name being mentioned. And no sooner had it been mentioned than we were all laughing, because most of us had asked one another in the same breath what had become of him.

It was Jack Price who was able to supply the information.

'For the last year or two,' he said, 'he's been living very quietly with his people in Norfolk. I heard from him only the other day.'

Mrs Storgate was interested.

'I wonder why he's chosen to efface himself,' she asked of nobody in particular. 'He was rather a lamb in his way. I used to adore that shiny black hair of his which always made me think of patent leather. I believe he owed half his invitations to his hair. I told him once that he dined out on it four nights a week.'

'It's as white as the ceiling now,' Price remarked.

Having spoken he seemed to regret it, and Mrs Storgate exclaimed:

'Oh, no! We're speaking of Simon Crutchley.'

'I mean Simon,' said Price unwillingly.

There was a faint stir of consternation, and then a woman's voice rose above the rustle and murmur.

'Oh, but it seems impossible. That sleek, blue-black hair of his! And he can't be more than thirty-five.'

Somebody said that he'd heard of people's hair going suddenly white like that after an illness. Price was asked if Simon Crutchley had been ill. The answer was Yes. A nervous breakdown? Well, it was something very like that. A lady who turned night into day all the year round and was suspected of drinking at least as much as was good for her, sighed and remarked that everybody nowadays suffered from nerves. Mrs Storgate said that Simon Crutchley's breakdown and the change in his appearance doubtless accounted for his having dropped out and hidden himself away in Norfolk. And then another conversational hare was started.

Instead of joining in the hunt I found myself in a brown study, playing with breadcrumbs. I had rather liked Crutchley, although he wasn't exactly one of my own kind. He was one of those quiet fellows who are said colloquially to require a lot of knowing. In social life he had always been a detached figure, standing a little aloof from his fellow men and seeming to study them with an air of faint and inoffensive cynicism. He was a writing man, which may have accounted for his slight mannerisms, but he didn't belong to the precious, superior and rather detestable school. Everybody agreed that he was quite a good scout, and nobody troubled to read his books which consisted mainly of historical essays.

I tried to imagine Simon Crutchley with white hair, and then I caught myself speculating on the cause of his illness or 'breakdown'. He was the last sort of fellow whom one would have expected to be knocked to pieces like that. So far from indulging in excesses he had always been something of an aesthete. He had a comfortable private income and he certainly didn't over-work. Indeed I remembered his once telling me that he took a comfortable two years over a book.

It would be hard for me to say now whether it was by accident or design that I left at the same time as Price. Our ways lay in the same direction, and while we were lingering in the hall, waiting for our hats and coats, we agreed to share a taxi. I lived in the Temple, he in John Street, Adelphi. 'I'll tell the man to drive down Villiers Street,' I said, 'and up into the Strand again by the Tivoli, and I can drop you on the way.'

In the taxi we talked about Crutchley. I began it, and I asked leading questions. Price, you see, was the only man who seemed to have heard anything of him lately, and he was now sufficiently evasive to pique my curiosity.

'It's a queer and rather terrible story,' he said at last. 'There's no secret about it, at least I'm not pledged in any way, but I don't think poor old Simon would have liked me to tell it publicly over the dinner-table. For one thing, nobody would believe it, and, for another, it's rather long. Besides, he didn't tell me quite all. There's one bit he couldn't—or wouldn't—tell. There was just one bit he couldn't bring himself to describe to me, and I don't suppose he'll ever manage to describe it to anybody, so nobody but himself will ever have an idea of the actual sight which sent him off his head for six months and turned his hair as white as a tablecloth.'

'Oh,' said I, 'then it was all through something he saw?'

Price nodded.

'So he says. I admit it's a pretty incredible sort of story—yet somehow Simon Crutchley isn't the sort to imagine things. And after all, something obviously did happen to him. I'll tell you his story if you like. The night's young. Come into my place and have a drink, if you will.'

I thanked him and said that I would. He turned towards me and let a hand fall on my knee.

'Mind you,' he said, 'this is Crutchley's own story. If you don't believe it I don't want you to go about thinking that I'm a liar. I'm not responsible for the truth of it; I'm only just passing it on. In a way I hope it isn't true. It isn't comfortable to think that such things may happen—do happen.'

Twenty minutes later, when we were sitting in the snug little library in Price's flat he told me his story, or, rather, Crutchley's. This is it. You know the sort of work Crutchley used to do? If you don't, you at least know Stevenson's Memories and Portraits, and Crutchley worked with that sort of material. His study of Margaret of Anjou, by the way, is considered a classic in certain highbrow circles.

You will remember that Joan of Arc was very much in the air two or three years back. It was before Bernard Shaw's play was produced, but her recent canonization had just reminded the world that she was perhaps the greatest woman in history. It may have been this revival of interest in her which decided Crutchley to make her the subject of one of his historical portraits. He'd already treated Villon and Abelard and Heloise, and as soon as he'd decided on St Joan he went over to France to work, so to say, on the spot. Crutchley always did his job conscientiously, using his own deductive faculties only for bridging the gaps in straight history. He went first to Domremy, where the Maid was born, followed the old trail of that fifteenth century campaign across France, and of course his journey ended inevitably at Rouen, where English spite and French cowardice burned her in the market-place.

I don't know if you know Rouen? Tourists don't stay there very much.

They visit, but they don't stay. They come and hurry round the cathedral, gape at the statue of Joan of Arc in the Place de la Pucelle, throw a victorious smile at Napoleon Buonaparte galloping his bronze horse on a pedestal in the Square, and rush on to Paris or back to one of the Channel ports. Rouen being half-way between Paris and the coast the typical English tourist finds that he can 'do' the place without sleeping in it.

Crutchley liked Rouen. It suited him. It is much more sober and austere than most of the French towns. It goes to bed early, and you don't have sex flaunted before you wherever you look. You find there an atmosphere like that of our own cathedral cities, and there is a great deal more to see than ever the one-day tourist imagines. Crutchley decided to stay on in the town and finish there his paper on Joan of Arc.

He found an hotel practically undiscovered by English and Americans—l'Hotel d'Avignon. It stands half-way down one of those narrow old-world streets quite near the Gare de la Rue Jeanne d'Arc. A single tramline runs through the narrow street in front of its unpretentious fagade, and to enter you must pass a narrow archway, and through a winter garden littered with tables and chairs to a somewhat impressive main entrance with statuary on either side of the great glass-panelled doors.

Crutchley found the place by accident on his first day and took dejeuner in the great tapestried salle a manger. The food was good, and he found that the chef had a gift for Sole Normand. Out of curiosity he asked to see some of the bedrooms.

It was a hotel where many ate but few slept. At that time of the year many rooms were vacant on the first floor. He followed a chambermaid up the first flight of stairs and looked out through a door which he found open at the top. To his surprise he found that it gave entrance to a garden on the same level. The hotel, parts of which were hundreds of years old, had been built on the face of a steep hill, and the little garden thus stood a storey above the level of the street in front.

This garden was sunk deep in a hollow square, with the walls of the hotel rising high all around it. Three rows of shuttered windows looked out upon an open space which never saw the sun. For that obvious reason there had been no attempt to grow flowers, but one or two ferns had sprung up and a few small tenacious plants had attached themselves to a rockery. The soil was covered with loose gravel, and in the middle there grew a great plane tree which thrust its crest above the roof-tops so that, as seen by the birds, it must have looked as if it were growing in a great lidless box. To imagine the complete quietude of the spot one has only to remember how an enclosed square in one of the Inns of Court shuts out the noise of traffic from some of the busiest streets in the world. It did not occur to Crutchley that there may be something unhealthy about an open space shut out entirely from the sun. Some decrepit garden seats were ranged around the borders, and the plane tree hid most of the sky, sheltering the little enclosure like a great umbrella. Crutchley told me that he mistook silence and deathly stillness for peace, and decided that here was the very spot for him to write his version of the story of Jeanne d'Arc.

He took a bedroom on the same level, whose high, shuttered windows looked out on to the still garden square; and next day he took a writing-pad and a fountain-pen to one of the faded green seats and tried to start work. From what he told me it wasn't a very successful attempt. The unnatural silence of the place bred in him an indefinable restlessness. It seemed to him that he sat more in twilight than in shade. He knew that a fresh wind was blowing, but it won not the least responsive whisper from the garden. The ferns might have been water-plants in an aquarium, so still they were. Sunlight, which burnished the blue sky, struck through the leaves of the plane tree, but it painted only the top of one of the walls high above his head. Crutchley frankly admitted that the place got on his nerves, and that it was a relief to go out and hear the friendly noise of the trams, and see the people drinking outside cafes and the little boys fishing for roach among the barges on the banks of the Seine.

He made several attempts to work in the garden, but they were all fruitless, and he took to working in his bedroom. He confessed to me that, even in the afternoon, he felt that there was something uncanny about the place. There's nothing in that. Many people would have felt the same; and Crutchley, although he had no definite belief in the supernatural, had had one or two minor experiences in his lifetime—too trifling, he said, to be worth recording—but teasing enough in their way, and of great interest to himself. Yet he had always smiled politely when ardent spiritualists had told him that he was 'susceptible'. He began by feeling vaguely that there was something 'wrong', in the psychical sense, with the garden. It was like a faint, unseizable, disagreeable odour. He told me that he did not let it trouble him greatly. He wanted to work, and when he found that 'it' would not let him work in the garden, he removed himself and his writing materials to his room.

Crutchley had been five days at the hotel when something strange happened. It was his custom to undress in the dark, because his windows were overlooked by a dozen others and, by first of all turning off the light, he was saved from drawing the great shutters. That night he was smoking while he undressed, and when he was in his pyjamas he went to one of the open windows to throw out the stub of his cigarette. Having done so he lingered, looking out.

The usual unnatural stillness brooded over the garden square, intensified now by the spell of the night. Somewhere in the sky the moon was shining, and a few stray silver beams dappled the top of the north wall. The plane tree stood like a living thing entranced. Not one of its lower branches stirred, and its leaves might have been carved out of jade. Just enough light filtered from the sky to make the features of the garden faintly visible. Crutchley looked where his cigarette had fallen and now lay like a glow-worm, and raised his eyes to one of the long green decrepit seats. With a faint unreasonable thrill and a cold tingling of the nostrils he realized that somebody was sitting there.

As his eyes grew more used to the darkness the huddled form took the shape of a woman. She sat with her head turned away, one arm thrown along the sloping back of the seat, and her face resting against it. He said that her attitude was one of extreme dejection, of abject and complete despair.

Crutchley, you must understand, couldn't see her at all clearly, although she was not a dozen yards distant. Her dress was dark, but he could make out none of its details save that something like a flimsy scarf or thick veil trailed over the shoulder nearest him. He stood watching her, pricked by a vague sense of pity and conscious that, if she looked up, he would hardly be visible to her beyond the window, and that, in any event, the still glowing stub of cigarette would explain his presence.

But she did not look up, she did not move at all while Crutchley stood watching. So still she was that it was hard for him to realize that she breathed. She seemed to have fallen completely under the spell of the garden in which nothing ever stirred, and the scene before Crutchley's eyes might have been a nocturnal picture painted in oils.

Of course he made a guess or two about her. At the sight of anything unusual one's subconscious mind immediately begins to speculate and to suggest theories. Here, thought Crutchley, was a woman with some great sorrow, who before retiring to her room had come to sit in this quiet garden, and there, under the stars, had given way to her despair.

I don't know how long Crutchley stood there, but probably it wasn't for many seconds. Thought is swift and time is slow when one stands still watching a motionless scene. He owned that his curiosity was deeply intrigued, and it was intrigued in a somewhat unusual way. He found himself desiring less to know the reason of her despair than to see her face. He had a definite and urgent temptation to go out and look at her, to use force if necessary in turning her face so that he might look into her eyes.

If you knew Crutchley at all well you must know that he was something more than ordinarily conventional. He concerned himself not only with what a gentleman ought to do but with what a gentleman ought to think. Thus when he came to realize that he was not only spying upon a strange woman's grief, but actually feeling tempted to force himself upon her and stare into eyes which he guessed were blinded by tears, it was sufficient to tear him away from the window and send him padding across the floor to the high bed at the far end of the room.

But he made no effort to sleep. He lay listening, waiting for a sound from the other side of those windows. In that silence he knew he must hear the least sound outside. But for ten minutes he listened in vain picturing to himself the woman still rigid in the same posture of despair.

Presently he could bear it no longer. He jumped out of bed and went once more to the window. He told himself that it was human pity which drove him there. He walked heavily on his bare feet and he coughed. He made as much noise as he was reasonably able to make, hoping that she would hear and bestir herself. But when he reached the open window and looked out the seat was empty.

Crutchley stared at the empty seat, not quite crediting the evidence of his eyes. You see, according to his account, she couldn't have touched that loose gravel with her foot without making a distinct sound and to re-enter the hotel she must have opened a door with creaking hinges and a noisy latch. Yet he had heard nothing, and the garden was empty. Next morning he even tried the experiment of walking on tiptoe across the garden to see if it could be done in utter silence, and he was satisfied that it could not. Even an old grey cat, which he found blinking on a window ledge, made the gravel clink under its pads when he called it to him to be stroked.

Well, he slept indifferently that night, and in the morning, when the chambermaid came in, he asked her who was the sad-looking lady whom he had seen sitting at night in the garden.

The chambermaid turned towards the window, and he saw a rapid movement of her right hand. It was done very quickly and surreptitiously, just the touch of a forefinger on her brow and a rapid fumbling of fingers at her breast, but he knew that she had made the Sign of the Cross.

'There is no lady staying in the house,' she said with her back towards him. 'Monsieur has been mistaken. Will Monsieur take coffee or the English tea?'

Crutchley knew very well what the girl's gesture meant. He had mentioned something which she held to be unholy, and the look on her face when she turned it once more in his direction warned him that it would be useless to question her. He had a pretty restless day, doing little or no work.

You mustn't think that he already regarded the experience as a supernatural one, although he was quite well aware of what was in the mind of the chambermaid; but it was macabre, it belonged to the realm of the seemingly inexplicable which was no satisfaction to him to dismiss as merely 'queer'.

Crutchley spoke the French of the average educated Englishman, and the only other person in the house who spoke English was the head waiter, who had spent some years in London. His English was probably at least as good as Crutchley's French, and he enjoyed the opportunity of airing it. He was in appearance a true Norman, tall, dark, and distinguished-looking. One sees his type in certain English families which can truly boast of Norman ancestry. It was at dejeuner when he approached Crutchley, and, having handed him the wine list, bent over him confidentially.

'Are you quite comfortable in your room sir?' he ventured.

'Oh, quite, thank you,' Crutchley answered briefly.

'There is a very nice room in the front, sir. Quite so big, and then there is the sun. Perhaps you like it better, sir?'

'No, thanks, said Crutchley, 'I shouldn't get a wink of sleep. You see, none of your motor traffic seems to be equipped with silencers, and with trams, motor-horns, and market carts bumping over the cobbles I should never have any peace.'

The waiter said no more, merely bowing, but he looked disappointed. He managed to convey by a look that he had Monsieur's welfare at heart, but that Monsieur doubtless knew best and must please himself.

'I believe I'm on the trail of something queer,' Crutchley thought. 'That chambermaid's been talking to Pierre. I wonder what's wrong or what they think is wrong.'

He re-opened the subject when the waiter returned to him with a half-bottle of white wine.

'Why do you wish me to change my room, Pierre?'

'I do not wish Monsieur to change his room if he is satisfied.'

'When I am not satisfied I say so. Why did you think I might not be?'

'I wish Monsieur to be more comfortable. There is no sun behind the house. It is better to be where the sun comes sometimes. Besides, I think Monsieur is one who sees.'

This seemed cryptic, but Crutchley let it go. Pierre had duties to attend to, and, besides, Crutchley did not feel inclined to discuss with the waiter the lady he had seen in the garden on the preceding night.

During the afternoon and evening he tried to work, but he fought only a series of losing battles against distraction. He was as incapable of concentration as a boy in love. He knew—and he was angry with himself because he knew—that he was eking out his patience until night came, in the hope of seeing once more that still figure of despair in the garden.

Of course, I don't pretend to understand the nature of the attraction, nor was Crutchley able to explain it to me. But he told me that he couldn't keep his thoughts off the face which had been turned away from him. Imagination drew for him a succession of pictures, all of an unearthly beauty, such pictures as he had never before conceived. His mind, over which he now seemed to have only an imperfect control, exercised its new creative faculty all that afternoon and evening. Long before the hour of dinner he had decided that if she came to the garden he must see her face and thus end this long torment of speculation.

He went to his room that night at eleven o'clock, and he did not undress, but sat and smoked in an arm-chair beside his bed. From that position he could only see through the window the lighted windows of other rooms across the square of garden shining through the leaves of the plane tree.

Towards midnight the last lights died out and the last distant murmur of voices died away. Then he got up and went softly across the room.

Before he reached the window he knew instinctively that he would see her sitting in the same place and in the same attitude of woe, and his eagerness was mingled with an indescribable fear. He seemed to hear a cry of warning from the honest workaday world into which he had been born—a world which he now seemed strangely to be leaving. He said that it was like starting on a voyage, feeling no motion from the ship, and then being suddenly aware of a spreading space of water between the vessel and the quay.

That night the invisible moon threw stronger beams upon the top of the north wall, and the stars burned brighter in a clearer sky. There was a little more light in the well of the garden than there had been on the preceding night, and on the seat that figure of tragic desolation was limned more clearly. The pose, the arrangement of the woman's garments, were the same in every detail, from the least fold to the wisp of veil which fell over her right shoulder. For he now saw that it was a veil, and guessed that it covered the face which was still turned from him. He was shaken, dragged in opposite directions by unreasonable dread and still more unreasonable curiosity. And while he stood looking, the palms of his hands grew wet and his mouth grew dry.

He was well nigh helpless. His spirit struggled within him like a caged bird, longing to fly to her. That still figure was magnetic in some mighty sense which he had never realized before. It was hypnotic without needing to use its eyes. And presently Crutchley spoke to it for the first time, whispering through the open window across the intervening space of gloom.

'Madame,' he pleaded, 'look at me.'

The figure did not move. It might have been cast in bronze or carved out of stone.

'Oh, Madame,' he whispered, 'let me see your face!'

Still there was no sound nor movement, but in his heart he heard the answer.

'So, then, I must come to you,' he heard himself say softly; and he groped for the door of his room.

Outside, a little way down the corridor, was one of the doors leading into the enclosed garden. Crutchley had taken but a step or two when a figure loomed up before him, his nerves were jerked like a hooked fish, and he uttered an involuntary cry of fear. Then came the click of an electric light switch, a globe overhead sprang alight, and he found himself confronted by Pierre the head waiter. Pierre barred the way and he spoke sternly, almost menacingly.

'Where are you going, sir?'

'What the devil has that got to do with you?' Crutchley demanded fiercely.

'The devil, eh? Bien, Monsieur, I think perhaps he have something to do with it. You will have the goodness, please, to return to your room. No, not the room which you have left, sir—that is not a good room—but come with me and I shall show you another.'

The waiter was keeping him from her. Crutchley turned upon him with a gesture of ferocity.

'What do you mean by interfering with me? This is not a prison or an asylum. I am going into the garden for a breath of air before I go to sleep.'

'That, sir, is impossible,' the waiter answered him. 'The air of the garden is not good at night. Besides, the doors are locked and the patron have the keys.'

Crutchley stared at him for a moment in silent fury.

'You are insolent,' he said. 'To-morrow I shall report you. Do you take me for a thief because I leave my room at midnight? Never mind! I can reach the garden from my window.'

In an instant the waiter had him by the arm, holding him powerless in a grip known to wrestlers.

'Monsieur,' he said in a voice grown softer and more respectful, 'the bon Dieu has sent me to save you. I have wait to-night because I know you must try to enter the garden. Have I your permission to enter your room with you and speak with you a little while?'

Crutchley laughed out in angry impotence.

'This is Bedlam,' he said. 'Oh, come, if you must.'

Back in his room with the waiter treading close upon his heels, Crutchley went straight to the window and looked out. The seat was empty.

'I do not think that she is there.' said the waiter softly, 'because I am here and I do not see. Monsieur is one who sees, as I tell him this morning, but he will not see her when he is with one who does not see.'

Crutchley turned upon the man impatiently.

'What are you talking about?' he demanded. 'Who is she?'

'Who she is, I cannot say.' The waiter blessed himself with quick, nervous fingers. 'But who she was I can perhaps tell Monsieur.'

Crutchley understood, almost without surprise, but with a sudden clamouring of fear.

'Do you mean,' he asked, 'that she is what we call a ghost, an apparition'

'It matters not what one calls her, monsieur. She is here sometimes for certain who are able to see her. Monsieur wishes very much to see her face. Monsieur must not see it. There was one who look five years ago, and another perhaps seven, eight. The first he make die after two, three days; the other, he is still mad. That is why I come to save you, Monsieur.'

Crutchley was now entirely back in his own world. That hidden face had lost its fascination for him, and he felt only that primeval dread which has its roots deep down in every one of us. He sat down on the bed, trying to keep his lips from twitching, and let the waiter talk.

'You asked Yvonne this morning, sir, who is the lady in the garden. And Yvonne guess, and she come and tell me, for all of us know of her. Monsieur it all happened a long time ago—perhaps fifty—sixty years. There was in this town a notary of the name Lebrun. And in a village half-way from here to Dieppe is a grand chateau in which there live a lady, une jeune fille, with her father and her mother. And the lady was very beautiful but not very good, Monsieur.

'Well, M. Lebrun, he fall in love with her. I think she love him, too—better as all the others. So he make application for her hand, but she was aristocrat and he was bourgeois, and besides he had not very much money, so the application was refused. And they find her another husband whom she love not, and she find herself someone else, and there is divorce.

And she have many lovers, for she was very beautiful, but not good. For ten years—more, perhaps—she use her beauty to make slaves of men. And one, he made kill himself because of her, but she did not mind. And all the time M. Lebrun stayed single, because he could not love another woman.

'But at last this lady, she have a dreadful accident. It is a lamp which blow up and hurt her face. In those days the surgeons did not know how to make new features. It was dreadful, Monsieur. She had been so lovely, and now she have nothing left except just the eyes. And she go about wearing a long thick veil, because she have become terrible to see. And her lovers, they no longer love, and she have no husband because she have been divorce.

'So M. Lebrun, he write to her father, and once more he make offer for her hand. And her father, he is willing, because now she is no longer very young, and she is terrible to see. But her father, he was a man of honour, and he insist that M. Lebrun must see her face before he decide if he still wish her in marriage. So a meeting is arrange and her father and her mother bring her to this hotel, and M. Lebrun he come to see them here.

'The lady come with them wearing her thick veil. She insist to see M. Lebrun alone, so she wait out there in the garden, and when he come they bring him to her.

'Monsieur, I do not know what her face was like, and nobody know what pass between him and her in that garden there. Love is not always what we think it. Perhaps M. Lebrun think all the time that his love go deeper than her beauty, and when he see her dreadful changed face he find out the truth. Perhaps when she put aside the veil she see that he flinch. I only say perhaps, because nobody know. But M. Lebrun he walk out alone, and the lady stay sitting on the seat. And presently her parents come but she does not speak or move. And they find in her hand a little empty bottle, Monsieur. . . .

'All her life she have live for love, for admiration, and M. Lebrun, he is the last of her lovers, and when he no longer love it is for her the end of everything. She have bring the bottle with her in case her last lover love her no more. That is all, monsieur. It happen many years ago, and if there is more of the story one does not remember it to-day. And now perhaps Monsieur understands why it would be best for him to sleep to-night in a front room, and change his hotel to-morrow.'

Crutchley sat listening and staring. He felt faint and sick.

'But why does she—come back?' he managed to ask.

The head waiter shrugged his shoulders.

'How should we know, Monsieur? She is a thing of evil. When her face was lovely, while she live, she use it to destroy men. Now she still use it to destroy—but otherwise. She have some great evil power which draw those who can see her. They feel they must not rest until they have looked upon her face. And, Monsieur, that face is not good to look upon.'

I had listened all this while to Price's version of Crutchley's story without making any comment, but now he paused for so long that at last I said:

'Well, that can't be all.'

Price was filling a pipe with an air of preoccupation.

'No,' he said, 'it isn't quite all. I wish it were. Crutchley was scared, and he had the sense to change to a room in the front of the house, and to clear out altogether next day. He paid his bill, and made Pierre a good-sized present in money. Having done that, he found that he hadn't quite enough money to get home with, and he'd used his last letter of credit. So he telegraphed for more, meaning to catch the night boat from Havre.

'Well, you can guess what happened. The wired money order didn't arrive in time, and he was compelled to stay another night in Rouen. He went to another hotel.

'All that day he could think of nothing else but that immobile figure of despair which he had seen on the seat. I imagine that if you or I had seen something which we believed to be a ghost we should find difficulty in concentrating our minds on anything else for some while afterwards. 'The horror of the thing had a fascination for Crutchley, and when night fell he began to ask himself if she were still there, hiding her face in that dark and silent garden. And he began to ask himself: "Why shouldn't I go and see? It could not harm me just to look once, and quickly, and from a distance."

'He didn't realize that she was calling him, drawing him to her through the lighted streets. Well, he walked round to the Hotel d'Avignon. People were still sitting at the little tables under the glass roof, but he did not see Pierre. He walked straight on and through the swing doors, as if he were still staying in the house, and nobody noticed him. He climbed the stairs and went to one of the doors which opened out into the high enclosed garden behind. He found it on the latch, opened it softly and looked out. Then he stood, staring in horror and fascination at that which was on the seat.

'He was lost then, and he knew it. The power was too strong for him. He went to her step by step, as powerless to hold himself back as a needle before a magnet or a moth before a flame. And he bent over her. . . .

'And here is the part that Crutchley can't really describe. It was painful to see him straining and groping after words, as if he were trying to speak in some strange language. There aren't really any words, I suppose. But he told me that it wasn't just that—that there weren't any features left. It was something much worse and much more subtle than that. And—oh, something happened, I know, before his senses left him. Poor devil, he couldn't tell me. He's getting better, as I told you, but his nerves are still in shreds and he's got one or two peculiar aversions.'

'What are they?' I asked.

'He can't bear to be touched, or to hear anybody laugh.'

The Running Tide

When my cousin Anstice was left a widow she had securities to the value of about two thousand pounds and the pension to which her husband's calling entitled her. I don't know how much goes to the widow of an Army captain who has met his death through an illness to which his military duties in no way contributed; but I know it isn't very much. As soon as her affairs had been put in order and explained to her, with great pains and at no small cost, by poor John's lawyers, Anstice began to see the necessity of doing something for herself.

Her intention of going into business was warmly applauded by all the wealthier members of the family who might otherwise have felt morally compelled to 'do something'. If one has money and poor relations it's very gratifying, I suppose, to see the latter develop a spirit of independence and get down to a job of work. But the difficulty was to find out what she could do and get her started on it, for Anstice, while being a woman of average common sense, had no special aptitude for anything, and knew nothing much about anything except lawn tennis, curry, and some of the Indian stations. I suppose in the circumstances it was quite natural that she should decide to run a private hotel or boarding-house. Women, when they go into business, love some kind of job in which they can be perpetually turning over ready money. It's a survival of that instinct which, as children, set them playing at keeping shops. Besides, Anstice liked company, and she confided in me her intention of charging such high terms that none but the nicest people would want to come and stay with her.

Most people were doubtful when they heard of her intention to pitch her camp in Lostormel. It was 'so far from London, my dear'. But I for one was able to perceive the common sense behind the intention.

I dare say most of you know Lostormel, on the south coast of Cornwall? In those days, four years ago, it had just been discovered as a holiday resort, through the faithful who visited it year after year not being able to keep their find to themselves. Anstice had visited the place with John in the August before his last illness, and had fallen in love with it, in spite of having found it overcrowded. There was very little hotel accommodation, every lodging in the town could have been let three times over, and she remembered having said at the time that anybody might make a small fortune by building and running another hotel. There was no doubt that she would have very little difficulty in keeping a full house throughout the summer. And, as she very pertinently said, the farther you got people to travel the longer they stayed.

Having decided on Lostormel, the next thing was to find a suitable house and get settled in it, and here Anstice confessed herself at a loss. She could run her boarding-house once it had got a start, but the preliminaries baffled her. She could drive the engine but didn't know how to get up steam.

Somebody must be with her to help and advise her until she was properly settled.

I don't know why everybody at once decided that I was the very person who ought to go and help poor, dear Anstice. I dare say my being a bachelor and having a year's leave at home may have had something to do with it. I was supposed to have no ties, you see, and have nothing to do but indulge a selfish inclination to treat a well-earned holiday as a holiday. However that may be, every uncle and aunt, and every cousin within range of a three-ha'penny letter, seemed suddenly to regard me as a potential authority on boarding-houses.

Anyhow, I took the line of least resistance and went. There were certain uncles and aunts whom it wouldn't have been politic to offend, and, besides, I knew and liked Lostormel. There's some bass fishing there that has to be tried to be believed, although nowadays it isn't what it was. So Anstice and I went down together in the early spring and put up at the Ship.

For the sake of those who don't know Lostormel, I'd better say at once that it's a typical small Cornish coast town of normally about four thousand inhabitants, cut in two by a river, up and down which the tides pass twice daily with the speed of racing greyhounds. It's a tricky river for visitors who like paddling about in small boats. They're liable to be left suddenly stranded on the mud until the tide turns, or shot out to sea like a pea out of a shooter, according to which way it happens to be flowing; and neither experience is worth having.

The town itself is very nearly as old as the hills which hem it in on all sides except the sea front. It's just like any other small Cornish seaside town—narrow streets, small and crazy-looking lime-washed houses, cobbles, stone steps going up precipitous slopes between one tier of houses and the next, and around everything a kind of atmosphere which gets into your head and is in itself a kind of tonic.

In Lostormel you suddenly realize that England isn't, after all, one huge stinking industrial town, seething with class-hatred and discontent. This is England, the real England, you think. For you find big, healthy men who haven't forgotten how to laugh, and all classes of people seem to mix together as naturally and happily as if we were already half-way through the millennium. As you thread your way through the streets you half expect to meet sailors with stocking caps and tarred pig-tails, men from Nelson's fleet, privateersmen, sly-faced smugglers, and even a stray pirate masquerading as Honest Jack.

For Lostormel was once a port of some consequence, but steam brought ruin to the town nearly a hundred years before petrol began to bring summer visitors. In the old days of the Wooden Walls men-of-war had rested in Lostormel harbour and merchantmen from all over the world had unshipped their cargoes on the quay. But with steam came the giant ships, and the little harbour—shallow enough when the tide was in, and mud when it was out—was given over to the fishing fleet.

Anstice and I spent long hours every day on house-hunting, which I soon regarded as a boring and unprofitable sport. Land values were going up and house values with them. All the houses on the market were too big or too small, or in an unsuitable position. Anstice was not easy to please. She wanted what she described as 'a darling old-world house with about fourteen rooms, facing the sea', and she wanted it at a price which put lines between the eyebrows of the local estate agents.

When you've given up hunting for a thing you often stumble across it accidentally. Every morning towards midday I used to sneak away from Anstice if I could and go and explore the wonderful old inns which you find in all the elbow-wide streets all over the town. There's a pub to every four adult inhabitants of Lostormel, and every one you go into is more curious than the last. And in the course of my explorations I found the Queen of India, the interior of which looked like the deserted cuddy of a condemned hulk. The bar, with its smoke-grimed match-boarding, was deserted on both sides of the counter when I entered it, or so I thought, and I was rapping with some money in the hope of attracting attention, when I was startled to hear a loud and sinister laugh behind me and a sudden rush of words.

'Joe Fox is a dirty old crimp! Yah-hah-hah! Joe Fox is a dirty old crimp!'

There is a fine old seafaring flavour about the word 'crimp'. I believe it means in the best technical sense a kind of boarding-house keeper who made a practice of doping and selling sailors to masters of ships about to embark. But I believe the term has been applied to other sorts of land-sharks. I started and turned to discover, of course, that the information about Joe Fox had been volunteered by a parrot.

He was a wicked old grey bird whose cage stood on a shelf just above a settle, and as I looked at him he chuckled hugely and began to mark time on his perch. I went over to him, of course, and as I approached he lowered his head to be scratched—and just missed my fingers with a vicious snap. I'd hardly started to curse him when I heard somebody stump into the room and a moment later a red-visaged, wooden-legged landlord, with a face which might have been carved out of teak, was standing beside me and thrusting his fingers through the bars.

'Gkk, Nero,' he said, and the parrot rubbed its beak against his stubby finger with every evidence of affection.

'What do you think of Joe Fox, Nero?' asked mine host.

'Joe Fox is a dirty old crimp!' screamed the parrot. 'Yah-hah-hah! Joe Fox is a dirty old crimp!'

'And what does Joe Fox live on?' Nero's master inquired.

'Sailors' blood, blast him, sailors' blood!'

I laughed.

'How on earth did you teach him that trick?' I asked.

'Me teach him, sir? I've taught him naught. He knew them words in answer to them same questions afore I was born. I've only kep' 'im up to it. I don't know how old Nero is, but he belonged to my grandfather who died in 'fifty-six. I've heard as Nero caught them sayin's off another bird my grandfather used to have what was old when this 'un was young. The two birds used to hang up side by side, and people 'ud come up and ask the old one what he thought of Joe Fox until this 'un got it off as pat as t'other.'

'That's interesting,' I said. 'Who was Mr Joe Fox, and how did he like it?'

Mine host winked at me.

'I reckon Joe Fox was dead before any parrot dared talk about him,' he said, 'I dunno when he lived, if he ever lived at all, but if he did he left a name behind him which don't smell very sweet to this day. When I was a lad old people used to tell tales about him that they'd heard from their grannies. They say he kept a pub here called The Running Tide, back along in the days when he was fighting the French in the daytime and doin' a bit of free-trading with 'em after dark. If all's true, more sailors was seen goin' into his house than was ever seen comin' out. But what with the press-gang comin' ashore here, and little quarrels between smugglers and Customs officers, and accidents bein' always likely to happen, sailor chaps was always disappearin' like.'

There it was again—that atmosphere of Nelson's time, and that rather jolly feeling one was always getting in Lostormel that the remote and picturesque past had crept up on to the very heels of yesterday. Mine host himself—I learned that his name was Jack Moggs—might have been a survivor of those splendid but doubtless uncomfortable days.

Well, finding that Jack Moggs was a good talker, and delighting in his society, I helped him to drink some of his own excellent beer; and after a while I asked him where I could find The Running Tide, for I liked the name of the inn and thought it might be worth a visit.

'Oh, bless your heart,' said Moggs, 'it ain't a pub now, and ain't been one since I can remember! It stands round the corner on the quay, and they just stores things in it now. Maybe they got the licence transferred to another house, maybe not. But the place 'ad a bad name through Joe Fox, and when the ships from foreign parts stopped comin' in there wasn't much trade for a house standin' there. I'll step along and show you where it is, if you like.'

I readily accepted his offer, and he stepped along—or, rather, stumped along—with me. I don't know why, but without seeing the place I had immediately got the impression that it might do for Anstice, but when I saw it the impression gained in strength. It was quite a good-sized house, and although thoroughly dilapidated it stood in an ideal position and had that air of antiquity which most visitors to Cornwall expect and require.

Inside I found a queer assortment of lumber, such as crab-pots, fishing-nets, anchors, small masts, and broken oars. Everything was in an abominable mess, and it would obviously cost a great deal to put the house into a habitable state; but to counterbalance that the price of it was likely to be proportionately low.

I told Anstice about it, and brought her along to see it in the afternoon. She came, saw, and was conquered. She loved its name—she intended continuing to call it The Running Tide in the event of her coming to occupy it—and she loved the bit of tradition about Joe Fox. She loved the old oak and teak inside, and she loved her vision of the house when her imagination showed her flattering pictures of what the decorators might be able to do with it. She was sure that it could be transformed into just the place which people would love to come and stay in, and as for Joe Fox—she asked me if it would be untruthful to boast that the house had once belonged to a smuggler or a pirate.

The next step was to find out who was the owner and how much he wanted for it. I managed both for her that very day. The price asked was even less than I had estimated, and a deposit was paid over within the week. I had then to make careful notes of everything Anstice wanted done to the exterior, and to the interior of every room, and to endure long interviews with Mr Ephraim Barbell, the head of a local firm of builders and decorators.

Getting the house habitable was, as I had warned her, a costly job.

Anstice was not short of ready money, for one of our uncles had stood guarantor for a pretty long overdraft, and it wasn't easy to get her to listen to any advice about economy. It was such a love of a house, she said, that it deserved to be made perfect. Besides, her contention was that if you intend rooking people for five or six guineas a week, you must give them a nice house to live in. It was a pretty dear place by the time she'd done with it, but I must say that the result almost justified the expenditure.

By the time the summer season had started the furniture was in. She'd given a London firm carte blanche, and they filled it with imitation antique stuff, and the house was ready to receive guests. Two of Anstice's women friends had booked rooms and were due to come on the last week in June. I thought then that I might safely say my Nunc dimittis, so far as Anstice was concerned, but she wouldn't hear of it. I'd been so sweet about everything, and now I must see her venture safely launched, and stay with her for the first few days after Mrs Lanson and Mrs Strode had arrived. We four were to hold a sort of house-warming. And she didn't want me to leave her until we were all sure that everything was running quite smoothly.

While the decorators were at work I'd been in and out the house two or three times a day, and I could not help noticing that out activities were creating a good deal of local interest. People came and stood around the house and watched what was going on with the half curious, half sympathetic look of people who have gathered after a street accident. The fishermen seemed specially interested, but they said very little except perhaps among themselves. The Cornish are not famed for being communicative to strangers.

One man, however, with whom I had got into conversation, told me that he didn't think the London lady would like the house. He said under pressure of questions that it was likely to be too noisy for her. Further questions elicited a fact of which I was already aware, namely, that the fishing fleet, which could only enter or leave the harbour when the tide was in, had sometimes to put out and return in the dead of night, and their comings and goings were not attended by deathly silences. But I thought that a minor inconvenience, and one from which other waterside hotels and boarding-houses had to suffer.

On the night before we were due to occupy the house, I went on an errand from Anstice to see that everything was in order. The servants were already installed, and were supposed to be preparing the house for our reception. We had just had the water laid on, and Anstice was fidgety in case it shouldn't be working properly. Besides which, I think she was anxious to find out how the servants were behaving.

We hadn't been able to get local servants, but that hadn't given us to think, for Lostormel shared in the pretty general scarcity. Anstice had engaged four, two girls from Plymouth, and a married couple named Hockley, who were to act as butler and cook respectively, and who had lately been in service in a big house near Liskeard.

The quay was deserted, for the tide was about half out, and the fishing fleet had gone to sea some hours since. It was a dark night, and it must have been after ten o'clock, so that I half expected to find that the servants had gone to bed. However, the way by which I came took me past the kitchen, and I saw both the windows lit up, and heard voices from within. And when I got round to the front of the house I saw that the dining-room window was dimly illumined and that somebody was standing just behind the glass. I went close to look and see who it was.

I'd seen the Hockleys before, and liked them well enough, but I hadn't encountered either of the two maids. Thus, when I stared at the woman who stood looking out of the window, I naturally supposed her to be one of them, and was momentarily staggered by Anstice's choice of servants.

I needn't particularize too much. The woman who stood in the window leering out upon the empty quay was obviously of the coarsest type which abounds everywhere where there are seafaring men. She was dark, and handsome enough after a bold and sullen-seeming fashion, and I saw her plainly enough to remember that she had heavy but plain rings bored through her ears. Seeing me, she gave me a brazen grin and jerked her head back a little, as if inviting me to enter.

This was a little too much. Angry, and yet half laughing at the ghastly mistake for which I imagined Anstice's innocence was responsible, I made quickly for the front door. Enter I did, and quickly, having a key, and I made straight for the dining-room to interview the lady who, it seemed, had been so unfortunate as to try her siren attractions on her mistress's cousin. Rather to my surprise I found the dining-room in darkness, and when I had switched on the electric light, I saw that it was empty. At the same moment, almost, the kitchen door opened, and a gruff voice asked who was there. This was Hockley's, and I called out to reassure him. He came through the passage from the kitchen to meet me in the hall.

'It's all right, Hockley,' I said, 'I've just come in to have a look round. One of the maids was in here just now'

He interrupted me quickly, and I noticed that his eyes dilated a little as he spoke.

'No, sir. Not one of the maids. We're all together in the kitchen.'

'Then it must have been a friend of one of you. There's no harm in your having friends here so long as they behave'

Once more he cut me short.

'Was she a big, dark woman with ear-rings, sir?'

'That's right. Who is she? I'm glad to know it isn't one of the maids. Whoever she is, I'm quite sure your mistress wouldn't approve of her being here.'

The man eyed me doubtfully.

'She looks like ' he began, and stopped abruptly.

'What our grandmothers would have called a painted hussy,' I said with half a laugh.

'Just so, sir. I've seen her myself. But I don't know who she is, or how she got into the house, or how she got out again. We'll go all over the house if you like, sir, but we shan't find her.'

I stared hard at him. 'I don't understand you. Somebody must know something about her. Haven't you questioned Mrs Hockley and the maids?'

He dropped his voice almost to a whisper.

'I haven't, sir. They wouldn't stay if they thought what I think. I was meaning to tell you, sir, but for the mistress's sake I daren't tell the others. We've all had one turn already which I've been trying to explain away. But the house is haunted, sir—I'm sure of that.'

You can imagine how annoyed I was. I could foresee poor Anstice's troubles being multiplied by an insoluble servant problem if such a tale were allowed to circulate.

'Oh, nonsense, nonsense, nonsense!' I exclaimed impatiently.

'Very well, sir. Just listen to this. Two or three hours ago, about an hour after high tide, when it was still quite light, we were sitting at supper in the kitchen, and we all of us heard a sort of screaming which sounded in the distance and yet seemed to come from upstairs. We thought a cat might have got into the house and couldn't get out, and I went out into the hall intending to go upstairs and see what it was. However, it wasn't necessary to do that, as

I could hear heavy footfalls coming down and the sound of something heavy being dragged across the floor of the landing. They reached the stairs—the footsteps and the dragging noise—and I looked up, and there was nothing there.

'I couldn't believe my eyes, but there it was. I thought I'd gone mad and just stood staring. The sounds came slowly downstairs, passed me where I stood in the hall, and then the door slammed without opening or shutting. I ran to it and opened it. There was nobody on the quay just in front, and yet after a moment came the sound of a big splash as if something heavy had been dropped into the water. It's my belief there's been murder done here, sir.'

It was my belief that somebody had been telling him about that possibly mythical character, Joe Fox.

'Well,' I said noncommittally, 'it all sounds very extraordinary.

Meanwhile, I think I'll satisfy myself that that woman isn't in the house. I know the front door is locked. Take me round to the back and I'll make sure of that. Then I'll have a look round.'

To cut that bit of a long story short, I searched the house thoroughly, but found no trace of that very unpleasant woman I had seen through the window. Hockley, it transpired, had seen her standing in the same place on the previous night. I swore him to secrecy. He was a good chap, as I was soon to discover, with a nerve of iron.

Anstice and I visited the house at about ten on the following morning with the intention of installing ourselves. The two paying guests were due to arrive by the afternoon train. Anstice made straight for the kitchen, and a moment or two afterwards I heard muffled sounds of surprise and lamentation. Then she came hurrying out to me.

'Isn't it a nuisance?' she exclaimed. 'Those two wretched girls from Plymouth have run away. They went out early this morning. What are we going to do now?'

I daren't look her in the face.

'Oh,' I said, 'I expect the Hockleys can carry on for a day or so until you get someone else. I suppose they didn't say why they went?'

'The Hockleys don't seem to know,' said Anstice.

Afterwards I interviewed Hockley. He said that they'd had trouble in the night after I'd gone, and that although his wife hadn't seen anything she was getting scared. The two girls had called him up in the night in a state of panic. All he could get out of them was something about 'the one-eyed sailor and the man with the knife'. They'd caught the first train back to Plymouth.

I didn't believe in ghosts, but I was on the way to conversion. There certainly seemed to be something radically wrong with the house. But still, from a mistaken sense of consideration,

I kept my thoughts from Anstice. Mrs Lanson and Mrs Strode duly arrived and we passed quite a happy and peaceful evening. At about half-past eleven I went to bed and slept.

I don't know what time it was when I woke, for I confess that I dared not reach out for my watch on my bedside table. I woke in an extremity of terror, drenched with perspiration, and not in the least knowing the cause of my mental torment. I found myself lying still and listening to the sound of the sea, and it must have been a minute or so before I became aware of another sound which mingled with it—a sound from close at hand and inside the house.

It was really a series of sounds, each one sharp and distinct, but running in a slow rhythm. Of course, one may translate nocturnal sounds to mean all sorts of unpleasant things. These seemed to me as if somebody, quite close at hand, were whetting a large knife with an expert and unpleasant air of thoughtful deliberation. And because I dared not believe that, I told myself it couldn't be. With one tremendous effort I got my head under the bedclothes and shut out those unpleasant noises. And after a while I fell asleep again.

It was on the following night that the worst happened. I went out fishing in the latter part of the day and returned in time to dress for early dinner. It was quite light. Anstice came out to meet me in the hall.

'We've had rather a scare,' she said. 'Some man's been into the house and taken something out. We were all sitting in the drawing-room just now when we distinctly heard a man dragging something downstairs and across the hall. Then the front door banged. I naturally thought it was Hockley who'd gone to throw some rubbish over the quay, and went out in the hall to waylay him when he came back and tell him he must use the back door for that sort of thing. But it seems he was in the kitchen all the time. Whom do you think it could have been?'

I could only shrug my shoulders.

'If nobody's lost anything I shouldn't worry,' I said, 'I dare say it was Hockley, and he remembered himself and returned by way of the back door.'

I was still hoping for the best, you see, and trying to keep things from the three women. I don't need to be told now that I was wrong to have done it. That night I didn't go to sleep at all. At about midnight, when I was just beginning to doze, I was jerked into full consciousness by a terrible and bloodcurdling scream. It was followed by the banging of a door and a rush of feet on the landing. Then came Mrs Lanson's voice, high-pitched and cracking with terror: 'There's a man with a knife in my room! There's a man with a knife in my room!'

I sprang out of bed, just as I was, in my pyjamas, and ran out on to the landing. Mrs Lanson stood there in her nightdress, her face a mask of terror, and modesty flung to the four winds of heaven.

'He's looking for someone—a man with a knife!'

Before I could move another scream rang out, this time from Mrs Strode's room.

'Help, help, help! He's in here! He's in here!'

I made a rush for Mrs Strode's room, and Mrs Lanson dived into mine. There was nothing in Mrs Strode's room except Mrs Strode herself. She was sitting up in bed gripping handfuls of bedclothes and staring straight before her out of dilated eyes.

'Where is he?' she cried. 'Where is he?'

'The man with a knife?' I made myself ask.

'No, no. A sailor. A sailor with a patch over one of his eyes. He was crawling about on the floor in an agony of terror, looking as if he were trying to hide. . . . Oh, don't go! Don't leave me alone! Take me with you!'

That was enough for all of us. We camped out in the drawing-room for the rest of the night, and presently the Hockleys joined us. What had really happened to them I don't know, except that Hockley afterwards told me they'd seen murder done, and Mrs Hockley sobbed and shivered and whimpered all night.

Fortunately it was a very short night, and when light came Anstice and I returned to the hotel at which we had been staying, taking Mrs Lanson and Mrs Strode with us. And later in the day I dismissed the Hockleys, paying them something above their month's wages, which they well deserved. Anstice, who had come off lightest of any of us, wisely decided never to spend another night in that house. Nor did she, and nor did I.

I suppose the explanation's simple enough if one accepts the hypothesis that such things can happen. I haven't the least doubt that it was a house to which sailors were once decoyed and afterwards robbed and murdered and their bodies given to the outgoing tide. At least, one of these evil deeds has left an ineradicable impression upon the house. Thus I am sure that I saw the decoy, that Mrs Lanson saw the murderer, and Mrs Strode saw the victim. Anstice sold the house at only a small loss to a retired naval man, who said he didn't believe in ghosts. She was perfectly frank with him, but he insisted that phenomena of that sort—in which he protested that he didn't believe—would be an additional attraction.

However, I think he believes in ghosts now, for he did not stay very long, nor has the house been inhabited since. It stands empty to this day, save for the crab-pots and nets and masts which have found their way back, and already it is half in ruins again.

The Oak Saplings

I warn you,' said Mrs Upcott, 'that this isn't at all a pleasant story, but if you will have it I suppose you must. You will have to take my word for a great deal, but it was I who laid the information before a certain society whose functions are to investigate so-called psychic phenomena; and an account of those investigations and the subsequent discoveries may be read in Derwent's Phantasms of the Living and Dead and Other Demonstrations of the Spirit World. However, I won't spoil the story before I begin it by telling you what those discoveries were.'

We drew our chairs closer to the fire and settled ourselves comfortably to listen. Hunter, however, had something to say first.

'I've read that book,' he said, 'but of course I don't know yet to which case you refer.'

'Brindley Manor,' began Mrs Upcott; and Hunter interrupted her with an ejaculation. 'You know the story?' she continued smiling.

'Yes,' he said, 'I know it now, but the others don't and—well, it's time they did. I beg your pardon, but—I understood from the book that the society had to thank a certain Miss Goring for bringing the initial facts before their notice.'

Mrs Upcott smiled sweetly.

'So they had,' she said, 'but a woman changes her name when she marries, and my maiden name happens to have been Goring.'

There was a murmur of subdued laughter at Hunter's discomfiture, in which he joined. That was the last interruption. The story promised well, and we were anxious to hear it. Mrs Upcott told it with the practised air of one who had narrated the same tale many times before, scarcely faltering once nor halting to grope for any elusive word or phrase. Here is the story, very much as she recounted it.

I was the only girl in a fairly large family, for I had two elder brothers and four younger ones. My father was a doctor with a fairly good practice in a London suburb, but the size of his family and the necessity for keeping up a good appearance kept him in a state of financial anxiety. Educating six boys and a girl, and afterwards starting the six boys in life is no joke to a man of moderate means.

Although I am speaking of comparatively recent times, those were the days when old-fashioned people, such as my father, were averse to their daughters working for their living and making a career for themselves. The girls were supposed to sit at home and be an expense and burden to their parents, until some obliging young man came along and married them.

I am afraid I was not particularly in love with the idea of working for its own sake, but I did not want to stand in the way of my younger brothers, three of whom were already of public school age. My two elder brothers were working, but they were still a drain on the household coffers. When I was twenty I began to have serious quarrels with my father and mother. The only kind of work for which they considered me fitted, and which they considered suitable, was that of governess in a 'nice' family. And it was the last thing I intended being, whether the family were nice or not.

So I took secret lessons in shorthand and typewriting, and as soon as I was reasonably proficient I began to answer likely advertisements. And after a dozen or so disappointments I got just the job I wanted.

This was the post of companion-secretary to a Mrs Carr, of Brindley Manor, in Dorsetshire. She was in Town when I answered her advertisement, and she invited me to meet her at her club for lunch. She was a middle-aged widow with two sons, one in the Army and the other practising Law in London. She preferred living in the country, but, deprived of the company of her sons, she suffered from fits of loneliness. Also, she had begun to amuse herself by writing books, and needed secretarial help.

We liked each other on sight. I thought her very bright and companionable and clever. That, of course, was before I saw any of her literary work; and when I did I wondered why the fine clear brain and sparkling imagination which served her so well in social intercourse should cease to function as soon as she put pen to paper. She wrote the most arrant rubbish, and knew it; she was the joy of such reviewers as were allowed to indulge tastes for facetiousness and irony; but after all it kept her amused, and she could well afford to pay for the publication of her books.

My father and mother were quite pleased when I told them. It had never occurred to them that I might become companion-secretary to an authoress with a good country address. If they had dreamed that such congenial work was to be had, my possible ability to do it had never occurred to them. I went with their blessing.

I had expected my life with Mrs Carr at Brindley to be pleasant enough, and I enjoyed it even better than I had hoped. Brindley Manor was a stone-built Jacobean mansion of medium size standing in a small park, bounded off one side by a wild and rugged heath which is crossed by the road from Dorchester to Bridport. On the opposite side of the park was a small village consisting of half a dozen cottages, a post-office and an inn. The house was secluded enough, and I could understand Mrs Carr having felt lonely. For my part, though, I had seen so little of the country that I enjoyed every moment of my days and thought that subsequent boredom would be impossible.

Having got me there, Mrs Carr did not seem to require so very much of my company, except in the evenings. I think it comforted her to know that I was somewhere close at hand if I were wanted. No sooner was I installed than she started a new book, and, since she did not dictate, my presence while she was at work would have been a hindrance rather than a help. In the mornings I was generally free to amuse myself as I pleased, and after lunch I typed out the morning's product of Mrs Carr's communings with the Muse.

After that our time was occupied diversely according to Mrs Carr's arrangements. Sometimes we went out walking together, sometimes to a neighbour's to tea; sometimes people came in to tea. About once or twice a week Mrs Carr would invite guests to come informally to dinner and bridge.

It was all very quiet and very pleasant. Mrs Carr and I liked each other very much, and went about a good deal together, for most people were kind enough to include the secretary in their invitations to the employer. But I think I enjoyed my mornings most of all, when I was left to myself and free to ramble where I liked.

The time of the year was early spring, the hedges were all flecked with the green dust of leaf buds; little nests of pale primroses sheltered under mossy banks; faint mists of green, growing brighter each succeeding day, clothed the dark shapes of the coppices. Bird-song woke me in the mornings and birds sang to me throughout my walks. The weather was sometimes showery, but mainly fair, and I was able to go out on most mornings and see the whole pageant of early spring.

Nearly every day brought a fresh discovery: daffodils springing to coloured life in unexpected places; violets hiding in woods where presently the bluebells would be out; shining dandelions, with their own peculiar fragrance, half buried in short grass like luminous yellow mushrooms. I walked among these delights, fresh from the staleness and ordered monotony of Suburbia, and rode my fancy on a loose rein and dreamed—oh, just the things you would expect a girl of twenty to dream.

And then one morning I had a fright.

It was one of those perfect mornings which we always get in England, before spring decides that she was selfish in coming so early and thinks she had better see what poor old dying winter can do for another week or so. It might have been the middle of June instead of the end of March, so warm was the sun and so innocent of clouds was the sky. I had started out in the best of spirits, and if these gradually declined, it was only because of that languor which I always feel when the weather is precociously unseasonable.

The park was studded with coppices and small plantations, and I was walking through one of these when I felt suddenly so languid and weary that I sat down to rest on the bole of a felled tree. The coppice consisted of nut-bushes, silver birches, holly and heavy timber, and it had lately been thinned. Here and there open spaces surrounded the stumps of giant trees. The nut-bushes were still half naked, so that I could see around me for a considerable distance, and the sun poured straight on to the tree-trunk on which I sat.

I don't know how long I sat there, busy with my thoughts and basking in the sun, but I certainly didn't doze. My seat, although better than none, was not conducive to slumber. I only know that I gradually became aware of a whispered conversation going on close to me.

It took time for me to realize or to imagine that the soft sibilant sounds I heard were actually the whispering of human voices, and then, without moving, I listened intently—not with the intention of eavesdropping, but to try to determine from which direction the whispering voices proceeded. But even if I'd wanted to hear what they were saying I should have been disappointed. I didn't pick out a single word. It was just the whispering of two people and—yes—I knew that it was the whispering of two lovers. The voices, subdued and muffled though they were, were undoubtedly male and female. He was saying caressing things, asking lovers' questions—for His whispered speeches always ended on a note of interrogation. In Her voice there was a sort of crooning note of love and reassurance.

I must have sat and listened to this unintelligible conversation for some little time before I began to be amused and mystified. I wondered who the two idiots were, and why they had chosen the vicinity of a third person as the scene of a love passage. I was certainly big enough to be seen! So presently I looked behind me and then all around me, and instead of seeing anybody I found myself completely—and in the circumstances terrifyingly—alone. Among the half-clothed bushes and the shorn tree-stumps around me there was no cover for a child, much less for a man and woman.

At that moment the whispering ceased and there was an infinitesimal period of total and dreadful silence before I heard once more the voices of birds and insects. The sun shone but the world seemed to be standing still. It was as if Nature had allowed me a peep at one of her undiscovered and awful secrets, and now laughed silently into my blank and frightened face.

But no sooner had that feeling come than it was gone. I sprang up in a kind of nightmare panic and shattered the silence with my own cry. Then the birds went on singing, wings fluttered among leaves and pliant branches bent, the myriad tiny voices of the spring woods became audible once more. And in the midst of these pleasant and natural sights and sounds I stood rigid and inexpressibly afraid, knowing that I had had some experience outside the common lot of men and women.

I succeeded in my effort at pulling myself together. I told myself that the terror of that dreadful moment was caused by my own too active imagination. I dared not pretend otherwise. As for the whispering, I started a comfortable theory concerning the action of the breeze in young leaves and tendrils. But at the same time, since I had owned myself subject to such disturbing fancies, I knew that it would be madness to linger, so, outwardly calm, but with a quickened step, I continued on my way through the copse.

Two or three minutes later I appeared at one end of a long clearing, and, raising my eyes, I saw at the far end that which surprised, amused, and to a great extent relieved me. There, at the other end of the clearing, were my lovers, locked in each other's arms. No doubt they were the whisperers who had passed behind me, and somehow I had failed to see them when I looked. I lowered my gaze—I hadn't the effrontery to be caught staring at them—coughed loudly, and raised my eyes again.

Now although I did not and do not wear glasses my sight has always been bad for distances, and all through my life it has played me the queerest tricks.

An imagined black cat seen along the roadside has turned out on closer inspection to be an old boot discarded by a tramp; a bird in a tree has become a leaf of unusual size and shape lodged there by the wind. My treacherous sight had another surprise in store for me at that moment. I was spared the shock of seeing my ardent lovers vanish before my gaze, but as I stepped forward they sprang suddenly into focus and revealed themselves to be two oak saplings standing alone just inside the far end of the clearing.

I stood and laughed aloud at myself, really amused. Here was an example of what imagination could do. The whispering I thought I had heard had made me think of lovers, and that thought, conspiring with astigmatism, had created lovers for me out of two baby oaks!

The two saplings were on my line of march, and I examined them in passing. They were growing much too close together to allow of either of them becoming trees, and probably they were the result of acorns fertilizing right on the surface of the earth. Now that I was close to them it was ridiculous to think that I had mistaken them at a distance for a man and a girl.

I passed on, and came suddenly upon a brick building. No, my eyes didn't deceive me on that occasion, although I was considerably surprised to find a building of any sort there in the middle of the park. Closer inspection revealed it to be a cottage, built doubtless for the accommodation of a keeper or bailiff, and while I was still wondering if it were occupied I had a practical demonstration that it was. The back door opened, and out came a dusty old man in shirt-sleeves and a coarse apron to stare at me with a not too friendly inquisitiveness.

He was not at all a nice-looking old man. Although he was astonishingly agile he looked at least eighty years old. His hair was long and nearly white, and his beard short and white and straggly. An Adam's Apple, so large as to be almost a deformity, worked in his throat. His bared arms, although painfully thin, were sinewy and looked capable of astonishing strength. Altogether he was undersized and wizened, and looked like nothing so much as an aged monkey, with all a monkey's aptitude for strength, agility and treachery.

'What do 'ee want?' he asked abruptly, in a voice which was firm and truculent despite its having been worn thin by age.

'Nothing,' I answered, 'I am just walking through the grounds.'

He came closer and peered into my face, while his hands began unconsciously to brush grains of sawdust off his coarse apron.

'You're not one of they Carrs, are ye?' he asked at last.

'No,' I said, 'I am merely an employee.'

His expression grew more friendly.

'I might ha' known,' he muttered. 'You're gentry like me, not jumped up offal like them. You're one of the old nobility, the old county families. Don't tell me. I know.'

I was amused and, I suppose, a little flattered. So far as I was aware there was no blue blood in my veins, and I had sprung from sound and undistinguished middle-class stock on both sides. I began to say as much but he would not hear me.

'No,' he said, 'you're one of the old gentry—like me. Eh, you wouldn't think it to look at me, but I'm a Baylord. The world's turned turtle these last generations, but they'll need our stock again. I'm not educated—I've been a workman all my life—but that I know.

'You listen to me, Missie. The Carrs and folk like them began to get a grip on the land a hundred years and more ago. The world went mad on machinery, it shouted and screamed for machinery, and 'twasn't the gentry who made it, it was scum such as the Carrs. The gentry sat in their fine houses, and dined with their fine friends, and hunted and thought the world was going on for ever like it had been. But the scum was getting the money, and taking the labourers from the land, so the value of land fell, and the gentry found themselves getting poorer. I'm right, ain't I?

'Then the scum got the gentry to invest in their tin-and-tinsel companies, for the gentry wanted to get back what they'd lost. And gradually they lost what they had, and though the companies failed the scum grew fatter and fatter. And they took the fine houses and the parks and the farms away from the gentry, so the scum became lords and ladies and peers of the realm, and bought coats of arms and sent their sons to college—but they couldn't be anything else but scum. Eh, I'm right, aren't I?

'I'm a Baylord, Missie. My grandfather was born in yonder great house. He let them take everything from him—the little tin men from Birmingham—and he died in a cottage on the edge of his own land. There was little enough for my father—not enough to educate me, but enough, so I've heard, for him to drink himself to death. And here be I still, a Baylord on Baylord land, but a carpenter by trade. I've only my name and the Baylord blood, and them Carrs and their tin friends from Birmingham, they wouldn't have no truck with the likes of me. They think I'm dirt under their feet. Eh, but I think they're dirt under mine and I tell 'em so. Scum! Offal! Why do they let me live here on my own land? Ask 'em that! Eh, ask 'em that!' I suppose I ought to have said something in defence of Mrs Carr, but to tell the truth I was becoming distinctly nervous of this very unpleasant old man, and thought it best not to disagree with him. Unfortunately he took my half-hearted manner for encouragement and went on to say some very highly unpleasant things about the Carrs. This was followed by a eulogy of his own family, the sometime lords of the manor.

'Wait, Missie,' he said suddenly, 'and I'll show you something.'

He disappeared into the cottage and while I was thinking that the opportunity had come for me to beat a retreat he reappeared with extraordinary swiftness, and I was not heartened to see that he carried in one hand a long, old-fashioned, silver-hilted Highland dirk. His demeanour, however, was perfectly friendly.

'You see this, Missie? You see that crest on the blade? This little knife used to belong to one o' they Scots chieftains. An ancestor o' mine took it off him in the Scots wars,' time o' Cumberland, when they was trying to put a Scotch king back 'pon the throne. Once it guarded the honour of a Highland gentleman's house, and after that it helped guard the honour of mine.'

He gave me a leer of almost incredible horror, fraught with some loathsome and unexpressed meaning.

'Eh,' he said, 'it's guarded the honour o' my house—that little old knife!'

I muttered something and began to move away. To my relief he did not try to detain me, but stood fondling the dirk as a musician fondles some beloved instrument.

'Step this way again, Missie,' he said. 'You're one of the old gentry, and I like to see ye. Step this way and be welcome, but not after dark.'

I could think of nothing more unlikely than my being in that vicinity after dark. But he had begged a question which some urgent sense of curiosity compelled me to ask.

'Why not after dark?'

His eyes narrowed, the great Adam's Apple in his throat began to work, and he dropped his voice to a reedy whisper.

'There's company in the copse at night as you wouldn't like meeting. There's them that can't sleep because they lies hard and damp. You haven't a little old knife like this, to keep 'em off you.'

By the time I returned I considered that my morning's ramble had been rather unpleasantly eventful, but I decided to say nothing to Mrs Carr. Doubtless she knew all about old Baylord—if that were indeed his name—and the things he was given to saying about her late husband's family. I did not want to embarrass her and myself by letting her know that I had heard them from him. But three or four afternoons later I accepted an opportunity to allow the cat to escape gracefully from the bag.

I was walking with Mrs Carr through the very copse where I had had the queer and disturbing experience which I have just described. She had fallen to talking about the characteristics of trees, and we had laughed at discovering that we had not between us one ha'porth of botanical knowledge.

'Don't you think there is a lot of character in trees?' she asked. 'A fir is a tall lean aristocrat, and seems to know it. A silver birch is a young girl, white and virginal. An elm is a pompous, useless old thing. A beech, especially an old one, is a wicked hag, given to witchcraft. And haven't you noticed how some trees look masculine and others definitely feminine in their poise and in the spread of their branches?'

She paused and pointed, finding a subject for illustration ready to hand.

'Look at those oak saplings at the other end of the clearing. Isn't there something very suggestive of a woman in the one on the right, and of a man in the one on the left? Can you see what I mean?'

'Perfectly,' I laughed, in fact, when I was here a few days ago my eyes played me a trick and for a moment I thought they actually were a man and a girl. They're just the right height, you see, and'

'Oh,' exclaimed Mrs Carr, interrupting, 'so you've been here before. I was just going to tell you that I wouldn't have walked in this direction alone, for fear of meeting old Baylord. I hope you didn't encounter him.'

'I'm afraid I did,' said I.

Mrs Carr looked at me and laughed.

'Then I can guess what he had to say about us and about his own family. He's like old Durbeyfield in Tess only he's a bitter, sinister old wretch. I suppose he told you that he ought to be living at the manor and that my late husband's people are the last and most unpleasant word in nouveaux riches.'

'Something of the sort,' I admitted, 'but he was so obviously out of his mind that I didn't take much notice of him.'

'My dear,' said Mrs Carr, 'there's certainly something in what he says. The Baylords held the old manor for hundreds of years until they gambled it away. The Carrs have no illusions about themselves. They're one of the new families. My sons and I draw our incomes from mines in Nottinghamshire and factories in the Midlands which we have never seen nor wish to see. If it's our good fortune that the old order is changing it certainly isn't our fault. One couldn't, if one wanted to, stay the course of evolution, any more than one can stay the course of a river with his hand.'

'I wonder, said I, 'that you let the old wretch stay there and say such awful things about you.'

Mrs Carr halted as if she thought we had gone far enough, and had better retrace our steps before we met the subject of our talk.

'That's the difficulty,' she said. 'We can't be hard on him, because we really feel that we owe him some redress. He has one real and legitimate grudge against us. My late husband's elder brother, Michael, eloped with his daughter over thirty years ago. Nothing's been seen or heard of them since, and Michael's father disinherited him for doing it. I think the disinheriting touched old Baylord's pride and hurt him more than the loss of his daughter. But Michael Carr undoubtedly wronged him, and, knowing that, we can't turn him out. He's a wonderful old man in his way, but he can't live very much longer. He still works, you know—does odd jobs in carpentry for the local builders—and scorns the old age pension.

We don't charge him any rent, and he lives there entirely alone, but how he manages to exist I don't really know.'

I have already said how very unlikely it seemed to me that I should enter that copse after dark, which only shows how the most improbable happenings can spring from the simplest causes.

It happened that one afternoon about a week later Mrs Carr ordered the Daimler and went over to spend a little time with a very old lady who lived some ten or twelve miles away. She did not take me with her, for the old lady was very old indeed, tired easily, and was averse to meeting strangers. I was free for the afternoon and set out for a ramble in the country.

I walked further than I had intended, lost myself twice, and darkness fell before I found myself near home.

I was very nervous and upset for having stayed out so long. I knew that Mrs Carr would have returned by that time, and might be in want of my company, and I did not want her to think that I had begun to take unfair advantage of her kindness in giving me so much liberty. With the intention of getting back as soon as possible I entered the park at the nearest point, with the idea of cutting across it diagonally to the house.

I never had much bump of locality, and when I plunged into a copse I had no idea that it was the same one in which old Baylord's cottage was situated. Things look so different after dark, and although there was a clearly defined path through the copse I had no idea of where I was, save that I was heading in the right direction. I didn't know until I got into the clearing and saw the two oak saplings.

As soon as I saw them something happened to me, a shock and a kind of nausea such as one feels when being taken down too suddenly in a lift. An icy wind of terror blew over me, chilling the perspiration which seemed to spring on the instant out of every pore of my body. The two saplings had become suddenly transformed. They were a man and a woman who stood there clinging together, distinct in the meagre light of the night skies. It had happened as quickly as the flicker of an eyelid, but I knew in my frightened soul that the thing was no mere caprice of vision.

The two semi-transparent bodies seemed to clothe the two saplings. I could see stems and branches through that diaphanous bluish covering. It was like looking at living bodies through X-rays. I knew' without any doubt that I was looking at two tragic and disembodied spirits.

They were clothed after a fashion which passed before I was born. I recognized it from the pictures I had seen in old journals. The Man—I must still call them Man and Woman—wore a deerstalker cap, a coat cut shorter and trousers cut fuller than the fashion of to-day. The Woman wore a bonnet. Her bust was prominent, her waist pinched, her long, full skirt billowed out over the hips. Her silhouette stamped her as belonging to the period of thirty or more years ago'. They stood quite still, but struck in postures of inconceivable woe.

How long I had to stand and look at them I don't know. It may have been only for a second but I leave you to guess how long it seemed. I had previously heard and made loose usage of that phrase about people being held spellbound. I never use it loosely now. I struggled to escape as one on the brink of waking struggles to escape from a nightmare. And presently I burst the shackles and screamed and ran.

I ran straight for old Baylord's cottage which was close at hand. He was repulsive but he was human and he was at least alive. He heard my cries for help and came to his back door which he opened, peering out of it candle in hand.

'I've seen' I gasped, 'I've seen' and that was all I could say at first.

'Eh, it's you, Missie,' he said calmly, 'I warned 'ee not to come this way after dark. Eh, I know what you've seen, Missie. I've seen 'em often enough. It's me they're after. Later they'll come peepin' about the cottage—that's why I keep the window-blinds tight drawn. But they haven't got inside yet, Missie. Not yet!'

While he was still talking I had stumbled past him into his living-room. I have a vague memory of it being incredibly dirty and untidy, and lit only by the one candle which old Baylord held in his hand. I collapsed in the one chair and the old man closed and barred the door and set the candle down among some dirty and ruined crockery on the table. Then he stepped to the mantel-piece, picked up the silver-handled dirk which lay there, looked cunningly towards the door and the window, and uttered a whinneying, senile laugh.

Some of my courage returned with the closing of the door.

'Who—who are they?' I stammered, feeling that I ought to have asked who were they.

The old man drew nearer to me, still fondling the dirk.

'You haven't heard, eh? Ah, if some knew—if some knew! You haven't heard, eh, that I had a little girl once? Not unlike you she wasn't. You haven't heard that, eh?'

'I heard that you once had a daughter,' I managed to say.

He stared very hard at me.

'Oh! They told you! And what did they tell you, Missie?'

I was all to pieces and I found myself answering quite automatically.

'She ran away with one of the Carrs.'

He chuckled at that, looked sidelong at the knife and uttered a sinister giggle.

'Yes, they went off together—on a long journey. But it wasn't so far that they can't get back o' nights. And nobody knows where they went—except me. You've seen 'em, Missie. Where those two saplings stand, I make no doubt. Presently they'll be round here, peeping in at the windows, shuffling about the doors—tryin' to get in. Eh, but they haven't got in yet.'

He drew nearer to me and seemed to grow more confidential.

'I'll tell you, Missie. You're one of the old aristocracy, like me and that girl o' mine, and you'll understand. Long before you was born, it must have been. She took up along with young Michael Carr—she that was a great lady for all that her father was a poor carpenter, and him that was less than nothing. They used to meet secret-like about the woods, and I knew what it meant. She was just a village girl to him, fair game for the gentleman he thought he was.

'I was her father, Missie, and I asked her questions which she couldn't answer. All the answer that I got was a hanging of the head and a shifting of the feet. So then I knew for certain and I went to him—the haw-haw gentleman—and when I talked of marriage he laughed in my face. He laughed in my face—and me a Baylord!

'So they went on their long journey, Missie, and nobody but me knows where. I planted acorns over them, Missie, but they was too shallow and too close together ever to become trees, and the roots is fouled by the black heart of Michael Carr and the fool heart of my girl.

'And they've been after me all these years but they can't get me. I'm tough, I am. Creeping around the windows and the doors they come. Maybe they'll get me before long now, but I've made a fight of it—a long fight. But the sap in them saplings is running, and the youth of the world is strengthening with the spring, and I be getting weaker. Maybe I won't be able to keep 'em out much longer, Missie.'

Somehow I swallowed a scream. I must have been half-crazy by then, but the half-hidden meaning of his words had somehow pierced the dull casing of my brain.

'What happened?' I heard myself cry. 'What did you do?'

He looked at that which he held in his hands and sniggered again.

'What would you have done, Missie?' he asked in a low penetrating whisper. 'Me a gentleman born, and my girl a lady, and ruined by that toad who was less than nought. What would you have done in my place, Missie? What would you have done—if you 'd had this little old knife?'

I don't know how I got back that night. I can honestly say that I haven't the least recollection of it. I only know that I was in bed for a week, and that the doctor who was called in thought I was going to have brain fever.

When I was better I told Mrs Carr all about it and I learned in time old Baylord was already dead. He had been found dead in bed and his silver-handled dirk was found lying near the door, of which one of the panels had been chipped, as if he had flung it at somebody who entered the room.

After that Mrs Carr wrote to the secretary of the society I've already mentioned, and they sent two men down. And what they saw in the copse Mr Hunter has already read for himself. You can all read the rest in the book I told you about, for I don't want to talk of it. But to be very brief, they uprooted the two saplings and found mingled with the roots the remains of a man and a woman.

A watch, found in the man's clothing, was identified as having once belonged to Michael Carr.

The Blue Bonnet

If you did not know Colin Forshaw there is just a chance that you may believe this story. If you knew him there is no chance at all, because he was the last man in the world with whom you would have connected such a story as I am about to narrate.

He was rural dean, besides being vicar of Hollycote, a big bluff man, an active player of games, although then in middle life—the kind of country vicar who is inevitably called the Sporting Parson. You know the type, even if you did not know Forshaw himself—the type which seems to run to beef rather than to spirit. And that, to my mind, makes the affair seem all the more remarkable.

Hollycote is right out of the world, being four miles from a railway station and the same distance from any road coloured red on the map.

Forshaw grumbled about his seclusion and pretended to be bored, but he had friends enough, and I do not believe he could have been happy elsewhere. He enjoyed spinning about the countryside in his dilapidated 'tin Lizzie', catching trout in the Laydon, playing tennis and village cricket, yarning with village worthies, and joking with the younger generation. I never knew a man who had more relish for his pipe and his glass, and I have heard him bellow like a bull over stories which were not intended for drawing-room repetition.

I have heard men express doubts as to whether he believed what he taught—they were wrong in this—but never a grumble as to the way he performed his duties.

For the rest, he was comfortably married to one of those rare feminine 'good sorts', who, in spite of her six children and her life of retirement, had never degenerated into the faded dowdiness of the average 'vicar's lady'. She was smart, she still bore traces of beauty, and she could be amusing. I think she had brought him some money, and he had a little of his own, so that the great barracks of a vicarage, which would have embarrassed any poorer incumbent, was maintained without financial anxieties. And now you know something of the man and his circumstances I can tell my story.

It was on a perfect July evening, and we were fishing for trout in the pool below Piddingford's Mill. Honesty compels me to admit that we were worming. For this more reasons than one must be held accountable, and the first was that owing to much overhanging foliage, no man could have cast a fly over that pool. It was almost a work of art to throw a worm and a ledger between branches and brambles.

True, we might have walked on past the little nursery garden and into the open fields beyond, through which the stream went rippling and eddying over wide shallows, and tried our luck with a dry fly.

We had indeed done so earlier in the day, and taken one small brace between us—or, rather, Forshaw had taken the fish while I whipped the stream in vain. But to-night we were fishing for the larder, Mrs Forshaw having warned us that breakfast depended mostly upon our efforts. I was staying with the Forshaws and, besides me, they had their three youngest children and two servants to feed. Fresh fish was difficult to obtain, the nearest town being seven miles distant. It was, therefore, necessary for the Laydon to yield up generously to us.

We had not done badly. Five or six fish, averaging half a pound, lay on the grass behind us. The water was clear, after three weeks of fine weather, else, Forshaw assured me, our labours need not have lasted more than half an hour.

It was late and twilight. Taking Summer Time into consideration I suppose it must have been close on ten o'clock. A deep peace sheltered everything around us, and Nature seemed to have turned drowsy under her warm wings. Even the water which fell foaming from the top of the little sluice-gate beside the mill-wheel had a soothing voice which sang sleepily.

Opposite us across the pool was the sheer wall of the mill, and a few yards upstream, beside the sluice-gate, the old wheel caked with dry green weed. Behind us was a small nursery garden belonging to a cottage higher up on our own side of the stream, and on the young rose-trees the roses were already hanging their heads in sleep. The night air was still, save for faint intermittent breaths of breeze which stirred the prim, well-disciplined ranks of flowers and shrubs, and wafted to us faint blended odours which were the sweeter for being so subtle and so elusive.

'Time's getting on,' said Forshaw suddenly, breaking a long silence and looking instinctively at his watch, which had stopped some hours since. 'And we want at least another two or three.'

'Shall we try another pool?' I suggested. Neither of us had had a bite for about ten minutes.

He shook his head, if we can't get 'em here,' he said, 'we can't get 'em anywhere. Besides, considering the water's gin-clear, we haven't been doing so badly. I think I'll go up to the sluice and try in the rough water.'

The bank, where it rose close to the sluice and the higher level of the river beyond, was comparatively free from obstructions. Forshaw rose and left me, and a moment later I had a nibble and struck at and missed a fish. I had reeled in my line and was examining my bait when I heard Forshaw's voice.

'I've got one,' it said.

I looked up and saw his rod bent like the arch of the rainbow, and heard the squeal of his check winch.

'By Jove!' he exclaimed joyously, 'I'm into a whopper!'

I seized the landing net at once, jumped up, and hurried towards him. His reel was silent now, only the top of his rod nodded and strained, and far down in the pool a long bar of silver gleamed and disappeared and gleamed again.

'Beggar's making for those weeds,' said Forshaw, 'and if he isn't a two-pounder I'll eat him raw.'

The Laydon trout are not like those from the Thames and Kennet where monsters of fifteen pounds or more are not unknown. Nor are they like the trout from certain West-country streams where a pound fish is a phenomenon. A Laydon trout of two pounds is considered a fine fish. One weighing more than that enjoys much local celebrity. The record fish was one of two and three-quarter pounds, taken on a Devon spinner just after the mayfly season.

Within two or three moments we had a look at Forshaw's prospective capture. It leaped two feet out of the water, arched like a great whiting ready for the table. After the resultant splash I breathed relief to see the line still as taut as a fiddle string. The struggle then proceeded silently save for the tick-tick-tick of Forshaw's reel as the fish, boring grimly downstream, gained or lost an inch or two in its fight for life.

But Forshaw was too experienced to make any mistakes. In a few short minutes the battle was over, and the tired trout, already half surrendering, was close under the bank.

'It's a three-pounder if it's an ounce,' said Forshaw, with the level voice of a man determined to be calm while in the act of achieving the ambition of a lifetime. 'Be careful!'

We were close to the sluice-gate, and the bank was high, but the rod of the landing-net was some six feet in length, and by lying flat I could easily reach the surface of the water. I lay down, my left arm outstretched, waiting for Forshaw to manoeuvre the fish towards me.

As I lay thus I looked straight into an indifferent mirror made by the hurrying waters. There was I, with my head, shoulders, and one arm protruding over the bank. A little to my right I saw the reflection of Forshaw and his bent rod, almost as still as statuary. But that was not all I saw. Standing not more than half a yard behind me was a girl in a blue sunbonnet, her gaze directed straight upon Forshaw's profile.

I cannot describe her very accurately. You must understand that I only saw her reflection in water that heaved and eddied as if it boiled. Her dress was just a shimmering blur of white, or maybe cream or light grey. I could see her features even less clearly, but they gave me an impression of youth and soft-toned daintiness. In that light, colours were but faintly reflected, but I could swear that her sunbonnet was as blue as the Mediterranean on a cloudless day. I saw her without, at that time, troubling myself to wonder who she might be. I suppose subconsciously I assumed that she was some village girl who had stolen up to watch a large fish being landed. Next moment I saw nothing but the fish, for Forshaw had brought it within reach of the net, and two seconds later I had lifted it on to the grass.

'By Jove!' said Forshaw softly, and with that he unhooked the fish and lifted it breast high in his spread hands.

'Well,' I said as triumphantly as if I had caught it myself, 'what do you think of that?'

I suppose Forshaw could tell by my tone that I was not addressing him, for instinctively he turned and looked behind him. I turned, too, to smile at the girl in the blue sunbonnet, only to find that she was not there. She whom I had seen reflected in the water had vanished as completely and suddenly as—and more inexplicably than—the lady in the cabinet trick.

I must have stood staring as blankly and stupidly as an owl. On one side of us was the stream, and on the other the nursery garden, which could not have afforded cover for anything much larger than a rabbit. It is true that there were trees further down the bank, but she could scarcely have had time to reach them, even if she had chosen to indulge in the inanity of hide-and-seek with us. It happened so quickly. She was, and in a moment or two she was not. I shall never forget the queer sensation I had then. It gave me what the old women call a 'turn'.

Forshaw must have assumed that, after all, I was addressing him. Having seen that we were alone he concentrated all his attention on his capture.

'I'll wager anything that this is a three-pounder,' he said; 'and if it is it's the biggest fish that's been taken out of this stream within living memory.

Pity I shall have to confess that I took it on a worm.' And he smiled over it with the slow, rejoicing smile of the born angler.

'Now, where the devil could she have got to?' I asked myself aloud.

'Eh?' Forshaw set down the fish and regarded me curiously.

'A girl who was standing behind us a moment or two ago!' I explained.

'I didn't see anyone.'

'I did. I saw her reflection just as I was slipping the landing-net under that fish. Where on earth she could have got to'

I broke off, and Forshaw looked around him.

'Must have been mistaken,' he said.

'I wasn't.'

'What was she like?'

'I couldn't tell. The water was swirling so. She was wearing something light and flimsy, something white or almost white, and a blue sunbonnet.'

I saw Forshaw start so violently that I thought he had hooked himself. He turned away and looked towards the cottage beyond the sluice.

'She couldn't have gone in there,' I said. 'There wasn't time.'

'No,' he answered, as if he were thinking of something else; but for the time being he seemed to have forgotten all about the fish.

'Do you know who she is?' I asked.

'I didn't see her,' he answered sharply. 'How could you expect me to know?'

'But how the deuce she could have vanished as she did'

'Oh,' exclaimed Forshaw impatiently, 'is it worth worrying about?'

I had to admit that, in a sense, it was not; and yet I was troubled and bewildered. I stood looking down at the great trout, but my mind was engaged elsewhere. Then I looked up to see that Forshaw was hurriedly taking his rod to pieces.

'Why,' I exclaimed, 'we're not going, are we?'

'May as well,' said Forshaw, shortly.

'But I thought we wanted two or three more.'

'This fellow's worth half a dozen.'

There was something queer in Forshaw's demeanour. He seemed to have lost all the angler's natural joy in his capture. His face was grave. It was as if there had been some unfortunate happening to interrupt our fishing. I wondered for a moment if I had said anything to offend him, so dour and silent had he suddenly become.

It was but a few minutes' walk to the old vicarage, and instead of talking about the largest trout which had ever come out of the stream, talking volubly and repeating ourselves, as is the way of successful anglers, we said scarcely a word. I took my cue for silence from Forshaw, and I knew that the girl whose reflection I had seen in the water was responsible for his altered mood. I, too, was worried. The almost magical suddenness with which the young woman had disappeared savoured of the uncanny.

We were in the drive and had almost reached the front door when I asked a question.

'Do you know any young woman in the village who wears a blue sunbonnet?'

'Nobody,' he answered shortly. 'Nobody now.'

I reflected that it must have been some visitor to the neighbourhood. Since village girls have taken to trying to dress like ladies, ladies staying in rural districts occasionally wear the old-fashioned dress of country wenches.

We weighed the big trout on the kitchen scales, and found that it was just half an ounce over the three pounds. The domestic staff, numbering two, were loud and voluble in their admiration. Back in the hall Forshaw plucked me by the sleeve.

'Don't say anything to Georgina,' he said.

Georgina was Mrs Forshaw, and I knew exactly what he meant. I was not to mention the girl in the blue sunbonnet. So I held my peace until half an hour later, when Georgina went to bed.

Forshaw, being nearest the door, opened it for his wife, and then followed her from the room. He returned a minute or two later with glasses on a tray, and a great jug of beer drawn from a barrel which had so many X's on it that it looked like the postscript of a girl's letter to her first sweetheart. He poured out the dark brown liquor, handed me a full tumbler, and motioned to me to help myself from a great tobacco jar, with the open book and triple crown on one side, and the arms of 'Univ.' on the other. Then he sat down opposite to me, took a deep draught, and began meditatively to load his pipe. I was considerably younger than Forshaw and felt some delicacy in asking him what troubled him. But I knew that he was going to tell me. Suddenly he smiled, and his smile was mirthless and tight-lipped.

'It's strange that you should have seen her just as I was landing that big trout,' he said, it's always at times like that. She must be very proud of me, you know. Do you remember, two years ago, when I got that century against Parling? You were here for the week-end, I remember.'

I inclined my head.

'Yes, I remember. You got out to a rotten ball when you'd got exactly a hundred. I suppose, having got your century, and the match already won, you chucked your wicket away.'

Forshaw shook his head almost imperceptibly, it wasn't that,' he answered, i was unnerved. I don't know whether you would remember, but I completed my hundred with a single through the slips, and as everybody began to shout and clap I knew what had happened.

Young Rackstraw, from over at the blacksmith's, was my partner at the wickets. The noise was still going on when young Rackstraw took guard at the other end, and the bowler was half way to the crease, when Rackstraw drew away from the wickets and held up his hand. He waited a moment, then took guard again, and played at the next ball.

'While the wicket-keeper was lobbing it back I called out: "What was the matter then, Racky?" "Lady behind the bowler's arm, sir," he said. "Right in front of the screen. Girl in a blue sunbonnet." I had a look round the ground, and there wasn't a blue sunbonnet in sight. That was enough for me. Next ball I had was a half volley, and I played right outside it.'

I felt that he was talking to me in riddles.

'Sorry,' I said, 'but I don't quite follow you. I don't see why it should have upset you. But it seems you do know a girl who wears a blue sunbonnet. Who is she?'

'She is the only girl I ever loved,' said Forshaw simply.

I stared at him incredulously, and my bewilderment found vent in a short laugh. Here was Forshaw, the brawny country parson and ideal husband and father, the last man in the world likely to be involved in a scandal, calmly confessing his love for some village girl. I must have been very thick-witted, even then, in not understanding.

'Don't worry,' he said with a short laugh at the expression I wore, 'I'm not going to embarrass you with any tale of domestic unhappiness. As you can see for yourself, Georgina and I are perfectly happy. We have been lovers, and we have reached a state of peaceful friendship and understanding. But there is another love which is different, even in the beginning. Everybody thinks they have experienced that other kind of love—passion knows how to look virginal at times—but I solemnly believe that it is given to less than one in a thousand. To such a love, I think, Elsie Harper and I attained.'

I shifted uncomfortably in my chair. Experience has taught me to mistrust that sort of talk.

'But, good lord, Forshaw!' I exclaimed, isn't this rather dangerous? I mean—if she's living in the same village'

Mirth and sadness together seemed to kindle a light in Forshaw's very blue eyes.

'Don't distress yourself, old chap,' he said quietly. 'Elsie Harper doesn't live in the village now. At least not in the way you think. As a matter of fact, she's been dead these thirty years.'

'What!' I exclaimed, and nearly dropped my pipe. 'What do you mean?'

'I mean,' he answered in a low, level voice, 'that what you saw tonight is what is commonly called a ghost.'

I confess that I tingled all over. A queer shrinking took possession of me.

I don't believe it,' I heard myself say.

'Very well. Account for it in some other way. You saw the reflection of a girl in the water. When you looked up a moment or two later there was no girl there. Indeed, if a girl had been standing there I must have seen her myself. Whenever I enjoy any sort of personal triumph, in sport, or in anything else, somebody always sees her. To-night I caught the record trout for that water. She came to watch me land it. She was always so proud of me, poor little angel!'

He was so sincere that it would have been almost impossible to argue with him.

'Do you ever see her?' I asked in a low voice.

He shook his head slowly.

'No, I never see her. It's always others. It's part of my punishment, I suppose, for—for once having not believed. But others see her, and I take it for a sign. I'm very thankful for that.'

I drank some beer and relit my pipe which had gone out.

'Has she—often been seen?' I stammered.

'Oh, perhaps a dozen times all told. I could give you all the instances. Once she appeared in church on a Sunday evening while I was preaching a sermon on one of the Commandments. It was a good sermon, though I say it who shouldn't. Sermons don't often influence people, but I learnt afterwards that the little weight which my words threw into the scale prevented a man and a woman from committing an act of criminal folly. Next day old Joliffe—he's the people's warden—asked me who was the girl in the blue sunbonnet who was sitting right under the pulpit. She was in the front row of pews so that nobody could see her face. And nobody seemed to see her come in or go out.'

'It's perfectly amazing!' I muttered. 'Would it be paradoxical to say that I don't doubt you, and yet I can't believe you?'

He laughed like his old self at that.

'Yes, I can understand. And yet you saw her!'

'You haven't yet told me who she was,' I reminded him.

'Ah! She was a girl in the village here. She lived in that cottage opposite the mill. Her father kept the nursery. I used to know her as a boy. My uncle had the living here in those days, and I used to spend half my holidays with him. The old man was a bit of a democrat, and encouraged me to play with the village children. I used to play cricket with Elsie's brothers. We had a practice net up on the further lawn in those days. Elsie never came to the vicarage, but sometimes I used to have tea with her brothers. That's how it all began, I suppose.

'I dare say I loved her from the very first, after some shamefaced, boyish fashion. At least, I was always showing off in front of her, and, strangely enough, she never saw that, and looked up to me with a sort of awe and was proud of everything I did. I was at a public school in those days, and a mighty superior young pup. When I was fifteen I started playing cricket for the village in the holidays, and when I made thirty-four against Murlford—and hit a six right over the hedge, where that stile is now—it was the happiest half-hour of my life, because she was looking on. That six shot was perfect timing, but in those days I preferred to call it brute strength. I strutted and preened myself before her as I never strutted and preened myself before anybody else.

'Still, it wasn't until I went down after the end of my first year at Oxford that I realized I loved her. I spent most of the long vac. with my uncle here. I was twenty then, and a devil of a fellow. I'd played in the Freshers' match and twice for the 'Varsity, although I didn't get my Blue until two years later. I was the cheap hero of every village match down here; there was nobody in the district who could stand up to me at lawn tennis; I was nearly half as good a fly-fisherman as I thought I was; and I had an indulgent mother who let me spend almost as much as I wanted to spend.

'I could tell by every glance I had from Elsie that she worshipped the ground I walked on and looked up to me as if I were some sort of demi-god. This encouraged me to posture more than ever, although I will swear that it was not frank admiration on the one side and flattery on the other that was the basis of the love between us. Although she was a child and I was a cub, I will swear that there was more in it than that—more than I could convey to any living man. I believe that some unknown law of Nature destined us for one another; but laws of Nature are often thwarted and—dis aliter visum.

'When we had discovered that our troubled spirits found rest and attainment while we stood clasped together, giving kiss for kiss, we used to meet along the river bank of an evening. I would go out and fish until she joined me, and after that I would only pretend to fish. She thought there was nobody in the world who could throw a fly like me. One day I saw her wearing a blue sunbonnet, and after that I would never let her wear any other kind of head covering on a sunny day; it so suited the rustic grace and beauty of her. I didn't want her to pretend to be a lady and dress like one. I wanted her to stay forever as she was, a little wild rose with the dews of morning on her. Somehow I could never imagine her growing old. That, I believe, is the case with most lovers; but regarding her I was right, for she never did. We were to be married, if you please, as soon as I came of age.

'It was her father who discovered the true state of affairs between us. I should have been, to say the least, a good match for his daughter from his point of view, and I know from what he told me later that never for a moment did he make the mistake of supposing that our love was other than innocent. But he was one of God's own honest men and, having questioned Elsie, he went to my uncle, the old vicar, and laid the facts before him.

'My uncle was democrat enough, but he did not lack worldly wisdom, or what passes for such. I was already destined for the Church and he had some ambition for me. They don't make bishops of men who have married into the peasantry. My uncle tackled me and there was a royal row. I could only babble such things as most youngsters of that age might be expected to babble about their first loves. Poor old man, I can forgive him now. He Communicated with my mother, and there were more rows. My mother, in the true spirit of those times, urged me to remember my distant kinship with certain scandalous but titled families. My extreme youth, some highly improbable Norman blood, and the risk of breaking a mother's heart, were all referred to in turn, but I stood firm.

'After much bickering, and some high words they struck a bargain with me—the usual sort of bargain. Would I wait two years without seeing Elsie or communicating with her? If our love were genuine and lasting it would stand the test of two years, and if at the end of that time we still wanted to marry, nothing would be done with a view to preventing us.

'That is a trappy test for young people. They feel that in declining to accept such terms they are tacitly admitting that they are not so sure of their own or each other's mind. In nine cases out of ten such a test is a triumph for parental wisdom, in that the young people discover that their affection was purely ephemeral and transitory.

'I saw the trap but I laughed at it and accepted the terms. I was so sure of Elsie and of myself. I am quite sure that if Elsie had lived we should have startled our elders by demanding that they should keep their side of the bargain.

'She died fifteen months later. My uncle relented at the last, and when it was known that she couldn't live, he wired to me at Oxford. I got an exeat at once and went down, but I was an hour too late. I only got her last message to me from her poor old father. "Tell him," she said, "that I shall always be near him and watching over him, and whatever he does I shall see, and be as proud of him as I always was, until we meet again."

'I don't care to remember the days and weeks and months that followed. I was like a madman. I cursed all my people for keeping us apart for those fifteen months which never could be given back to us. After nearly thirty years it still hurts me to think and to remember. There was no comfort, only a sort of aching pathos, in her last message to me. How could she watch over me when she was dead? And her talk about meeting again was children's talk. For in my bitterness I suddenly found that I believed in nothing—no religion, no continuity, no hereafter.

'For nearly two years I gave up all thought of taking Orders. Until then I had been content to swallow dogma, accepting it all as a comfortable philosophy. But now that I had tasted bitterness and loss, I could not believe that Elsie still existed as a conscious entity and that at the end of time we should be reunited. She was dead in some dreadful final sense of being dead, as irrevocably lost as the flame of a blown-out candle. Like thousands of others, I wanted a sign, you see.

'I had my first sign when I pulled a woman out of the Thames at Richmond. The usual mob collected. We were giving her artificial respiration when somebody standing by remarked on having seen a girl in a blue sunbonnet on the edge of the crowd. Now people at Richmond do not wear sunbonnets. A short while later, when I was at home with my mother and the news arrived that I had taken a First, one of the maids swore to seeing a girl in a blue sunbonnet standing outside the door, and she described Elsie with the most minute accuracy. A girl in a blue sunbonnet appeared at the cricket ground at Edgbaston, and mysteriously disappeared again, on the occasion when I got sixty not out against Warwickshire on a sticky wicket.

'In all my triumphs, whether they were worthwhile or merely such showy performances as Elsie had once delighted in, a girl in a blue sunbonnet was seen for a moment or two. I never saw her myself. I take it that faith was still demanded of me in that I have always had to accept the word of others. That faith I came to give gladly, for I could not suppose that the inexplicable appearances and disappearances of a girl in a blue sunbonnet were merely a series of strange coincidences. And through thus being assured that Elsie still lived, I found my lost way back to faith and hope.

'That is all that there is to be told. I am quite sure it was Elsie whom you saw tonight. I am quite sure that she is with us now, and has heard every word which has passed between us. And that is why I claim to be one of the happiest men alive.'

But the story does not end there. For my own sake I wish it did, but for Forshaw's sake I am glad that there is a word or two to add.

In the following winter I lost my poor old friend. Double pneumonia and pleurisy carried him off. He had contracted his last illness through going out on a bitter evening and sitting through half the night in wet clothes beside a sick man. I went down for the funeral, and to stay on for a day or two afterwards, since I had charge of some of his affairs which now had to be cleared up.

While I was there I heard a whisper in the village as to what young Rackstraw at the blacksmith's was supposed to have seen at almost the very time that poor Forshaw passed away. I questioned young Rackstraw and found him shy at first.

'They're all saying I'm daft,' he muttered shamefacedly.

'Never mind,' I said, smiling, i think you're sane enough.'

'Well, sir, you knows as parson died about seven in the morning? We all knew as there wasn't much hope for him. Just about seven that morning, when it was just getting light, I was passin' the vicarage on my way down to work.

I'd got past the gate when something made me look back, and there was parson coming out into the road. I couldn't believe my eyes at first and thought as he must ha' got better all of a sudden by a kind o' miracle.

'He wasn't alone. There was a girl with him, and she was dressed in summer white and wore a blue sunbonnet. A blue sunbonnet at this time o'year! I reckon it must ha' been the same lady as I saw once on the cricket ground.

'Neither of 'em seemed to see me. He had her by the hand and she was smilin' up at him and he was smilin' down at her. They was just like any young couple as you can see walkin' through the lanes on a summer evenin'; but I've never in all my life seen two as looked so happy.

'Then I lost sight o' their faces, for they turned to the left outside o' the gate, and, hand-in-hand, walked slowly towards the east, where the sun was beginning to rise.'

Through the Eyes of a Child

This was Mrs Hunston's story, prefaced by a little nervous and apologetic laugh, and told to the circle gathered round the fire after dinner.

'I'm sure you won't believe it,' she said, 'and I can't blame you. I certainly can't prove it. All those who could help to substantiate my words are dead, except, perhaps, Miss Clutton, and she may be for all I can say to the contrary. There's a stained-glass window in Propington parish church, an old newspaper cutting and two old steel buttons to lend—what's that dreadful word?—verisimilitude to what I am going to tell you. I can show you the newspaper cutting about the discovery of the body, and the buttons, whenever any of you like to come and see me; but the stained-glass window you'll have to take on trust unless any of you care to drive over to Propington in the next county and see it.'

Somebody facetiously forgave Mrs Hunston for not having the stained-glass window with her. She acknowledged the little joke with a broad smile.

'You'll have to take so much on trust,' she said, 'that a little thing like a stained-glass window shouldn't trouble you. And, of course, if anybody bothered to go and see it, it wouldn't prove anything. But if you really do want the story, and will promise not to be too rude about it to my face, I'll tell it with pleasure. I don't mind what you say behind my back. I shan't care because I shan't know.'

I have found it convenient to delete most of Mrs Hunston's self-interruptions and digressions; but the following is her own story, very much in the manner of her own telling:

When I was a small girl—I was about eight or nine, I suppose—my father, whose finances had always had a mercurial quality, made a sudden fortune on the Stock Exchange, and decided to retire while still almost a young man. He was fond of sport and of the countryside, and had always coveted the life of a country squire. That was how he came to buy the Propington estate, in Wiltshire. The Baxters, the biscuit people, have it now.

I think he decided on Propington because my mother was a Rivers, and born not ten miles away. In those days business people who bought big country properties were apt to be cold-shouldered by their longer-established neighbours, but my mother's people were strong enough in the county to insure against a frigid reception. As far as I can remember my parents were very popular from the beginning; at least we seemed to have a host of ready-made friends as soon as we arrived, including some uncles and aunts and cousins who were hitherto quite unsuspected so far as I was concerned.

Propington Hall was a big Elizabethan house, built of soft-toned red brick, and, like many other houses of that period, it was gabled and shaped like the letter E. It was the sort of house which no compiler of guide-books could resist describing as 'a rambling old manor'. It was a thrilling change to me after our old home at Hampstead, and I got lost in it several times before I learned to find my way about. It was surrounded by a deep dry moat, with a close-cropped lawn at the bottom. I don't suppose there had ever been water in it—I don't know where it could have come from, for one thing—but I liked to think that it had once been full and that prisoners had been thrown into it in that vague period which was so mysteriously called the 'good old times'.

The church was in the park, and quite close to the house. The main drive, which passed between the church and the house, was open to the public on every day of the year except one, when the village people couldn't go to church even if they wanted to, and the gates were locked to prevent it from becoming a right-of-way. I'm obliged to tell you all this, because of what follows.

In those days not nearly so many daughters of well-to-do families went to school as they do now. It was 'the thing' to have a governess until one was nearly old enough to come out, and then go to a finishing school—probably in Paris. Thus my father's determination to do the right thing, and my mother's ready acquiescence, provided me with Miss Clutton. I remember thinking her very beautiful, although quite old—she must have turned twenty— and I grew to be very fond of her, although to be sure we had our little quarrels. We played at work rather than worked, and she took me out walking a great deal and always seemed to be very surprised—although I soon ceased to be—when we met Mr Greyburn, the curate.

Mr Greyburn had second sight and a bicycle. At least, I know he had the latter, and I'm almost sure he had the former. Wherever we went Mr Greyburn and his bicycle would be sure to overtake us, sooner or later, or come flying to meet us in a cloud of dust, and always he would dismount and have a long talk with us, which I thought so kind of such a holy and such a busy man. And invariably on our return Miss Clutton, who had yellow hair and demure amber eyes, would remark that it would, perhaps, be as well if I refrained from mentioning the meeting, since people might otherwise think that Mr Greyburn was neglecting his parochial duties if he were always about on his bicycle.

There were a good many children of more or less my own age belonging to the neighbouring families, and I went out to tea quite a lot and gave schoolroom tea-parties which happened almost as often as my mother's at-home days. And when Christmas came round, bringing a lot of small boys home from their preparatory schools, I lived in a perfect riot of parties.

Of course, I had to give one of my own, and this was a proper evening affair, with dancing, games and forfeits, and a buffet supper consisting mainly of jellies, trifles and such things dear to the hearts—or should one say tummies?—of children. But the piece de resistance of the evening's entertainment was intended to be the engagement of Professor Rascallo. Professor Rascallo was, I believe, in ordinary and unromantic life, a hairdresser in Devizes named Goodridge. But occasionally of an evening, when he could get an engagement, he hired a dress-suit and became Professor Rascallo, the World-famous Prestidigitateur and Illusionist.

I remember very well the arrival of the professor. He was given a table to hold the necessary implements of magic at one end of the big drawing-room. Fronting this table chairs borrowed from all over the house were arranged in rows, and I went round, very importantly, as hostess, showing the other kiddies into their seats, smallest in front, and doing my best to arrange that everybody could see.

I needn't remind you that that period, the end of the 'eighties and the beginning of the 'nineties, was a terrible time for children's fashions. Little boys wore unmanly petticoats until they were four or five years old, when they were promoted to such unreasonable abominations as kilts or sailor suits. Upon slightly bigger boys were inflicted velvet costumes with ham-frill collars for their more auspicious occasions, and at my party there was more than one Little Lord Fauntleroy. Above them came the Olympians, clad in a fashion comparatively sane, in Etons and white waistcoats, and seeming to my childish eyes almost as grown-up as Captain Dodds and Mr Gervase Rivers, and one or two other grown-ups who had come in to help make the party 'go'.

Among the wretched small boys dressed in the fashion of the Cavaliers, was Harry Bligh-Page, the son of some near neighbours. He was extremely 'pretty' and girlish, and obviously proud of his finery. I couldn't imagine him wanting to roll about and get himself dirty like other boys, and I hated him for his effeminacy. Still more did I hate him, because my father and mother, seeing my aversion, teased me by pretending that he was my Little Sweetheart. Partly on that account I hated even having to speak to him. On this occasion, if you please, he turned up in green silk, with a wide lace collar which almost overlapped his shoulders.

Well, we all got settled into our places, and then my father brought on Professor Rascallo and introduced him in a speech which made us all laugh and gave us anticipatory thrills. The professor was a man of about fifty, who took the average barber's pride in a luxuriant growth of hair, which he wore rather in the fashion of a Fiji chieftain. He had also a very large moustache, which he had evidently trained like a creeper, and a dress-suit which fitted where it touched—as the saying is. I remember his face very well, and although I was too young to understand such things, I must admit, on looking back, that it was not the face of—well, shall we say a bigoted teetotaler?

However that may be, there was nothing to show at the beginning of his entertainment that he had called at the shrine of Bacchus on the way, to fortify himself against the strain of the evening's engagement. I don't suppose he was a very good conjuror, but we were not critical. Children in those days weren't; and anybody who could extract live rabbits from an empty hat, make eggs disappear through candle-flames, and produce the flags of all nations from his mouth was good enough for us.

The earlier items of his programme were carried through successfully enough, and then came a hiatus prior to the performance of some more elaborate trick. A little boy and girl, I remember, had been beckoned to the table to bear witness to something which was going to be done, and while they blushfully came out before the public gaze I looked over my shoulder to see how my guests were enjoying themselves, and distribute a smile here and there, as my gaze happened to be met. I was a very important young person for the evening, remember!

It happened that I looked through a lane of heads, craning to left and right, straight at one of the windows at the back of the room. The curtains had all been drawn before the party began, but one or two rough games had been played, and the curtain of the window at which I looked had been dragged aside. On the far side of the window, pressed very close against the glass, I saw a boy's face and the upper half of his body. He was dressed in green, and wore a wide frilled collar. Wait a moment! I know what some of you are going to say. If he were outside in the dark and I were inside in the light, how could I see the colour of his coat? I can't answer. All I can say is that I saw him as I've described him to you, and at the time I didn't think it particularly queer. To be honest and truthful, I thought little Harry Bligh-Page had gone exploring outside and hadn't been able to find his way back, and that he was trying not to miss the conjuror by peering in through the window.

If it had been any other boy I would have drawn attention to his plight. But I hated Harry, and with all the sensitiveness of a child, I dreaded the arch remarks of my father and mother—and others, for that matter—if I seemed to notice him at all. Being in some respects a hard-hearted little beast, I just turned my head and left him to his plight.

Well, Professor Rascallo, having satisfied his young witnesses that there was no deception, folded the gold hunter which he had borrowed from my father into a handkerchief, and then proceeded to smash it to pieces with a hammer. I concentrated my attention on what was happening. I knew that my father valued that watch, and I was wondering what he would say to Professor Rascallo, for I was sure that the watch could never be the same again.

Professor Rascallo made a neat job of folding up the handkerchief into which he had placed the wreckage of the watch. He then, with one seemingly miraculous movement, made a knot across the middle, and, holding the handkerchief up by two diagonal ends, began to swing it like a censer. Then he turned to the little girl whom he had called up from the spectators.

'Now, miss,' he said, 'as I swings this, I wants you to watch it carefully and repeat after me these 'ere magic words—umpty-dumpty-idas-midas. Would you mind sayin' them words, miss? Right? Are you ready?' He drew himself up, looking over the heads of all of us, and began again to swing the handkerchief. I remembered afterwards that he seemed to be looking straight at the window from which the curtain had been dragged.

'Now,' he began, 'just repeat after me, "Umpty" '

He got no further. His face froze. He stood still for a long moment staring straight over our heads as immobile as if somebody had thrust a pistol against his brow and dared him to move. Then he swayed like the pendulum of a clock and came down. His head struck the table with a crash, and my father's watch, perfectly intact, dropped out of the handkerchief and rolled to the feet of one of the children in the front row.

He was picked up and half carried away, amidst general consternation. Mother told us to sit still and then followed after the men. She came back after a minute to tell us that the Professor wasn't well, and that although it was nothing very serious he wouldn't be able to continue the entertainment. Captain Dodds, however, came back and sang us two funny songs, and then the boys were asked to put the chairs back alongside the wall for the resumption of games and dancing.

In the general commotion which followed I caught sight of Harry Bligh-Page and knew at once that it couldn't have been he whom I had seen on the other side of the window, for I was sure that none of my small guests had entered or left the room since the beginning of the conjuring entertainment.

After a while we all moved into the dining-room where the supper delicacies were laid out, and by that time I'd forgotten all about the little boy in green that I'd seen staring in through the window. I was too excited to trouble my head about him, although it did occur to me to wonder who he could be, since only Harry seemed to be wearing that particular colour.

As we crossed the hall I wanted to say something to Captain Dodds who stood talking to Gervase Rivers, and waited until I could put in a word without interrupting. They were not at first aware of my presence.

'Yes,' Captain Dodds was saying, 'he's all right now. Charles'—that was my father—'sent him home in the carriage. I warned Charles not to give him anything before the show. I could see that he was as drunk as a fiddler's lady-dog when he arrived.'

'All the same,' said Gervase Rivers, 'it's rather funny that he should have had that kind of delusion, because you know the old story'

It was just then that my close presence was discovered, my curls were pulled and I was asked what I wanted. I went on into the dining-room knowing quite well, of course, that they had been talking about the conjuror.

Two big fires were burning in the dining-room, one at each end, and it wasn't long before somebody complained of the heat. So a curtain was stripped aside from a tall casement window, which was pushed open a few inches and kept steady by a perforated bar which fitted into a knob on the sill.

Well, stand-up supper had been in progress for about ten minutes when I happened to glance at this half-open window and saw staring into the room from the outside a boy in green with a frilled collar—evidently the same boy that I had seen before.

On this occasion I was much nearer the window, and it was half open, remember; so consequently I had a better view of him. I saw at once that he was a stranger, and despite his elaborate clothes there was nothing of the 'party' aspect about him. His green coat was old and stained, his face grimy, and his hair very long and dishevelled. And he was gazing upon the crowd of happy youngsters inside the room with a wistfulness which went straight to my heart.

Now on Sundays I was given to read a kind of juvenile literature which in those days was considered proper for the Sabbath. The stories were always about extremely pious children who, apart from interfering in the most unwarrantable manner with the spiritual affairs of their elders, were extremely dull and almost invariably died in the end, after a lachrymose deathbed scene extending over at least two chapters. The motif was nearly always the same.

The hero or heroine was invariably a rich child who adopted a poor child as a protege, and brought much sunshine into a little life which was overcast by the shadow of a cruel stepmother who was addicted to gin and atheism.

I don't deny that in those days I used to enjoy such stories, and could always imagine myself in the part of heroine; but this was the first occasion that I had had, so to say, a chance. I ought to have pointed out the stranger and said: 'Mamma, there is a poor little boy outside, and he looks, oh! so sad.

May I not ask him in that he may share our harmless fun?' But even then I wasn't quite prig enough for that. However, I did approach the window to ask him what he wanted, with the intention of smuggling out some dainties to him. I guessed him to be some very poor boy who had been given the discarded 'party' clothes of some more fortunate youngster.

I must add that it didn't seem in any way extraordinary that some poor village child should have come right up to the house. The road which was open to the public on all but one day a year passed just outside between the west wing of the house and the church. It wasn't so extraordinary that village children, hearing that there was a party, should gather round and venture to peep in. What was extraordinary I didn't realize until a moment or two later.

I drew quite near to the boy outside the window. He saw me approach and smiled. I never saw such a haunting look of tentative friendliness. Then, when I was almost within arm's length of the window, his face convulsed in an agony of shyness, and he vanished like the flame of a match blown out by the wind.

I thought he had merely ducked down below the level of the sill, so I forced the window open to its fullest extent, knelt on the window-seat and peered down. And I looked straight down twenty feet into the bottom of the moat.

We were on the ground floor as, of course, I knew, but I'd forgotten all about the moat. And—the moat ran under the drawing-room windows, too; there was nothing but a sheer drop. I sprang back from the window, screaming, and was instantly surrounded by a crowd. I have a vague, confused memory of telling everybody that a poor boy had fallen into the empty moat and killed himself. There was a considerable to-do, I assure you, but every child was soon accounted for. Still, to comfort me, my father and one of the servants lit lanterns and walked around the moat, only to find nothing there.

It was then decided that I was ill and must go to bed. Unkind suggestions as to over-eating, and the fault bringing its own punishment, were broadly hinted at in my hearing. So I was led off weeping and disconsolate, a very poor sort of hostess, still protesting that a little boy had fallen into the moat and killed himself.

I cried myself to sleep that night, for there was something about that boy in green which attracted me very strongly; and I was quite sure that he must have been killed. In the night I woke suddenly to hear voices outside my door. They were my father's and Captain Dodds's.

'Oh, I shouldn't worry about a doctor yet,' Captain Dodds was saying reassuringly. 'See how she is to-morrow. It's over-excitement, of course, and unfortunately she heard me talking to Gervase about what that drunken barber thought he saw. He knew the story, of course. He admitted that afterwards. And that put the idea into her head.'

'It must have been that,' my father muttered. 'The Ropers never saw anything.'

'They hadn't any children. He's only supposed to be seen when there are children about, you know. But I shouldn't think about that. Don't for your own sake start a ghost scare '

'S-sh!' whispered my father, suddenly remembering, 'She sleeps in there, and she might still be awake.'

I wasn't awake very long, for the fragment of conversation didn't frighten me. I don't think I knew what a ghost was in those days. I was quite sure in my own mind that I had seen the same boy outside two of the windows over the moat, but I knew that to insist on this would be to court punishment, for my father and mother had no small sense of discipline. Once they said a thing was imaginary, imaginary it had to be.

So next morning I dressed as usual and went downstairs, and prudently said nothing, except, when asked, that I now felt quite well again.

That morning, when Miss Clutton and I set forth on our usual walk, I looked back at the house. I could easily identify the windows outside which I had seen the boy standing, but there was no ledge on which he could have stood—nothing but the sheer blank wall. However, that only puzzled me a little. Enough that I had seen him and wanted to see him again. I could not guess how he had got there, but boys were wonderful creatures in my estimation, and I was able to credit them with impossible climbing feats and all manner of incredible performances, so that when I saw him again - Oh, yes, of course I saw him again! I'm coming to that. Often I saw him about the house after dusk, but I could never get very close to him until once—the last time. Always he gave me that friendly, wistful, haunting smile, but he would never let me come near. I got to understand that this wonderful, strong, handsome boy was for some absurd reason afraid of Me! You've seen a dog that's been ill-treated and yet wants to be friendly, suspecting at the last moment the soft voice and snapped fingers of some new human acquaintance, and running from him in terror. The boy was just like that.

I often wondered who he was, and what he was doing in our house, but I said nothing about him. I didn't want to be told that I was ill and must go to bed, and I didn't want him to be driven away, which I thought might happen if I could induce others to believe in his existence.

Once I met him on the stairs and he turned and fled before me like the wind. I was just in time to see him enter my own room, and I ran after him. I thought the door must be open, but I found it wasn't, for I ran plump into it.

And my room was empty, for I searched everywhere.

The end came on an evening in February. Miss Clutton had taken me out to tea at the house of another little girl, and we were returning home through the park just as late twilight was turning to dusk. We were about half way to the house and had reached a spot where there was a thick plantation of trees on our left, when we heard the sound of a bicycle bell and the rattle of a loose mudguard, and the inevitable Mr Greyburn bore down upon us. He dismounted, asked me how I did, and began to talk to Miss Clutton.

Presently they lowered their voices and edged a little away from me. I, realizing that they wished to talk privately, withdrew myself a yard or two, and while I loitered, wondering how long the confabulation would last, I saw the Boy peering out at me shyly from behind one of the trees. I gave chase at once and without warning, and ran until I nearly dropped. Then two hundred yards away, I heard the crow of a disturbed pheasant, and realized the hopelessness of pursuit. I stayed and rested, and then made my way back, without hurrying, to the drive.

I found Miss Clutton and Mr Greyburn in a state of consternation, wondering what had become of me, and my frank confession that I had run after a little boy in no way improved matters. Run after a little boy! The idea! Whoever heard of such a thing!

Miss Clutton rated me soundly when Mr Greyburn had ridden on. It seemed that I was a very naughty little girl, and that she would report me to my mother as soon as we got home. I don't believe that she would have kept her threat if I had not said: if you do, I'll tell her all about you and Mr Greyburn.'

Poor Miss Clutton was furious. This was a challenge which she could not possibly ignore, so, on the moment of our arrival, she marched off to find my mother.

I was not present to hear the evidence. I was tried in my absence and found guilty, and brought up for judgment afterwards. My mother was grieved that a daughter of hers could be so forward and unladylike as to run after a little boy, particularly a little boy whose mother we didn't know, because that was the only kind of little boy who would be likely to be out by himself at that hour. The sentence was that I should go straightway and supperless to bed, and that I should remain a prisoner in my room until I had begged Miss Clutton's pardon.

I went off storming. I was never going to beg Miss Clutton's pardon. She was a beast. Everybody was a beast. I had a fine, noisy temper as a child, and it was because of this temper that I squalled and cried after flinging myself down in the arm-chair in my room.

My sense of justice was outraged, you see. I should not have minded much if I could have felt that I had done wrong. To me it seemed perfectly right and natural that I should run after that dear little boy whom I had seen so often about the house, and who seemed to want to be friends although he was so absurdly afraid of me. And yet I daren't even mention him for fear of being told that I wasn't well. And there was the professor, too. Look how they'd treated him for seeing the boy! They'd turned him out of the house and said he'd been drinking!

I held my hands to my face and rocked myself to and fro in an agony of impotent rage, and suddenly I felt—I shall never describe it—but I knew he was in the room with me.

I looked up out of my streaming eyes and saw him standing before me not more than two yards away, gazing at me with a compassion which melted my heart. Quite shamelessly I held out my arms to him.

'Little boy!' I whispered. 'Little boy! Everybody's cruel to me. I do love you, little boy!'

He gave me his smile of ineffable sadness and friendliness, but came no nearer.

'What's your name, little boy?' I asked.

His smile grew sadder, and he tapped his lips with a finger as if to tell me that he could not speak.

'Won't you come to me?' I pleaded. 'Be nice to me. Everybody else is so horrid, and I'm so miserable.'

And as I spoke the words I somehow knew that he felt the same. I saw his little face working as if he were trying to make up his mind. Then as swiftly as a bird alights he came and bent over me and kissed my face. The touch of him was a revelation. It was quite palpable and yet less substantial than water. I knew as quickly as thought could flash the light upon my startled little brain that he was not a child like myself and that he was not of this world. It wasn't for that, though, that a panic terror went through me like a cold wind and began to thunder in my brain. It was something beyond reason or control—the revulsion of living flesh from the touch of a naked spirit.

His own terror was simultaneous with my own, and equally violent. He sprang backwards with incredible swiftness and stared at me out of dilated eyes, his mouth set in a fixed grin of fear. And then—then the threatened eternity of that awful moment was ended. The door opened and Miss Clutton came in.

I don't know to this day if she saw him. She left us long before I was old enough to be told the whole truth. But she saw my face and sprang to me with a cry, gathering me into her arms.

'Darling!' she cried, 'Darling! What's the matter, darling?'

I managed to speak before I fainted.

'He went in there!' I cried, pointing. 'He went in there!'

And I knew that I had pointed at the blank face of a panelled wall.

I slept in Miss Clutton's room that night, and I never returned again to my old one. I was told next day that the workmen wanted to come in and do something to the room. I did not hear until I was almost grown up that they stripped away the panels and found a staircase in the thickness of the wall, leading to a small cellar under the moat. Nor did I hear anything about the coroner's inquest nor of the little coffin which was subsequently buried after dark. For in the cellar they found the skeleton of a child, and the perished rags which still covered it were identified at the inquest as having once been a boy's costume of the middle seventeenth century period. Two of the steel buttons were kept for me as a memento, and I have them still.

The discovery made sufficient stir to attract the attention of the newspapers, and it was generally assumed that the remains of poor little Rupert Thirkhill had at last come to light. And the story of Rupert Thirkhill is as old as the 'Babes in the Wood'.

In the seventeenth century and earlier it seems that some people named Thirkhill were lords of the manor. When Parliament took up arms against the king, the head of the family fought on the king's side, and after all had been lost at Naseby fled to France, leaving his infant son in the care of servants at the house.

The estate was confiscated and handed over to a brother who had fought for Parliament, and poor Rupert Thirkhill was brought up by an uncle and aunt who must have wished him well out of the way. There were Royalist risings and plots everywhere, and there was always the chance that the young Charles would return and win back his father's throne. In that event the estate would probably be given back to the boy's father, and with the boy out of the way the usurping brother would be in any event the natural heir.

Thus it happened that poor little Rupert disappeared and was never seen again. It was given out that he had run away, although everybody suspected that he had met with foul play at the hands of his uncle. But the fact was never proved, and after the passing of a number of years his death was presumed.

The inevitable ghost legend followed. Propington Hall was supposed to be haunted by the spirit of the poor murdered boy, but it was generally by children that he was seen, and unless there were children in the house he was not seen at all. It was always the presence of other children which raised that forlorn little child spirit—as if he liked to see them about his old home and yearned to join in their games.

I never saw him after that night, and I don't think he was ever seen again.

I don't know why. The ancients, of course, believed that a spirit couldn't rest while the body it once inhabited remained unburied. I don't think I shall trouble about what becomes of my body once I've left it, but who knows what whims we shall have in the Beyond? To be sure, we've all got our crotchets and unreasonable fancies in this life, haven't we?

My father and mother had a stained-glass window put into the parish church in Rupert Thirkhill's memory. It represented St Stephen, the boy martyr of Norwich. The vicar was High Church and raised no objections. My father and mother announced that the window came from me.

It's still there to be seen by anybody who cares, and underneath is a brass plate with the following inscription:

The gift of one child to the memory of another.
Ora pro Donatore ad Dominum Deum Nostrum.

Mr Garshaw's Companion

My excuse for telling you this story (began Gamer) is that my friend Jerry Wilson thoroughly believes it, and I can vouch for his honesty. If he's the last man in the world whom you would think likely to be mixed up in an affair of this sort, he's also the last man to swear to what he knows to be false. I can assure you that it's not a story that I want to believe, but I've got an uneasy feeling that there must be something in it. Anyhow, here it is, and you must please yourselves what you think.

Jerry Wilson was one of those men who learned to ride a horse during the War, and realized what he had missed through not having been taught as a small boy. He took up riding as naturally as a duckling takes to a pond, and when the War was over he found himself possessed of a new and expensive hobby.

He was in business in London. His business was not so extensive as to deny him a certain amount of week-day leisure, and he could just afford to hunt on an average one day a week throughout the season with packs whose territories could be quickly and easily reached by train from Town. His favourite hunt was that one in Sussex of which Lord Greenchurch was the Master.

I don't know how Jerry Wilson's Army riding-school style of horsemanship was suited to the hunting-field, but I don't suppose he was conspicuous. In all hunting districts so easily accessible from London it is nothing new to see stockbrokers and other dwellers in the City cutting the most extraordinary antics on horseback. And since visitors who hired local hacks and paid their Cap were tolerated rather than welcomed by the subscribers, Jerry Wilson made no friends in the district.

On a certain February day when the hounds were due to meet at Pirriedown Cross, Wilson, having communicated overnight with a local livery stable, took train in the early morning to Pirriedown station. The train arrived three-quarters of an hour late, owing to a dense fog which rose suddenly, unexpectedly, and thickened with obstinate persistence as the journey continued, so that long before it exploded the fog-signal outside Pirriedown station it was obvious that there would be no hunting that day.

Wilson found himself a ghost among other dark ghosts walking disconsolately down the open platform in an atmosphere of the colour and texture of dirty chiffon. He was at a loose end. The day was Saturday, and he had made no other plans for the week-end. Since he was in any event free of the City on the following day he had intended to stay the night at the George instead of dragging his tired limbs back to London. Now he was undecided, and at the booking-office he inquired about a return train, only to be told that in the normal course of events one was not due for an hour and a half, and now goodness only knew what time it would get in and what time it would reach Victoria.

He looked out through the open door leading into the station yard and saw the fog wreathing like the smoke from a witch's chimney. No, he decided, he would not wait unknown hours in the miserable waiting room and spend the best of the day in a crawling and fog-bound train. There was always the George, with its quite reasonably comfortable lounge and drawing room, hot meals, and the chance of intelligent conversation with some new acquaintance.

At the worst he could find a book and a comfortable chair by a fireside, and take a day's complete rest. And if the fog didn't lift by nightfall and allow the trains to run normally, with only the usual stops at every station, he could stay the night as he had originally intended.

The George is one of those half pretentious roadside hotels which cater for motorists in the summer and keep open during the winter to comply with the licensing regulations. Its public rooms are furnished mainly with imitation antiques. It has a smoke-room in which the wealthier and more gentlemanly topers of the district seek sanctuary from their wives. Its landlord complains that he loses money during the summer and hobnobs with Ruin throughout the winter. In fact it is just an average English country hotel of the type which makes a foreign tourist homesick, and rouses all his patriotic fervour.

Wilson felt his way to it through the fog, walked into the lounge and entertained himself with a copy of the Tatler, which was almost old enough to be placed in a dentist's waiting-room, until the time arrived when the People Who Never Shall Be Slaves are legally permitted to quench their thirsts. The bars and the smoke-room then filled with disappointed sportsmen, some of them still in riding-kit, and Wilson went into the smoke-room in the hope of finding congenial company.

He drank little at ordinary times, but like many other men he was inclined on occasions to drink from sheer boredom when there seemed nothing else to do, and when he found himself in the company of others who were at the same loose end. That morning he owned to taking a sufficient quantity of whisky and soda to make himself sleepy, so that after lunch he felt sleepier still. He found on a shelf in the lounge a copy of a detective novel left there by a summer visitor, took it to a comfortable arm-chair before the fire, and fell asleep over the first chapter.

When he woke it was almost dusk, the fog outside having helped to deaden the waning daylight. He was wakened by the entrance of a tall thick-set man in a light brown tweed coat, a stock, riding-breeches and gaiters. The newcomer walked ponderously to an arm-chair on the side of the hearth opposite to where Wilson was sitting, sat down heavily and emitted a long sigh.

Wilson looked at him sleepily and recognized him. He had seen the man several times in the hunting-field. He was rather a strange-looking fellow, Wilson thought, with a grotesquely if not unpleasantly ugly face. He was a man of about fifty with a dome-shaped head which was nearly bald, and the pendulous jowl and protruding under-jaw of a bulldog. He hunted regularly, and Wilson had already categorized him as belonging to those whom he described as 'Up-stage and County'. He nodded tentatively and received a nod and a smile in return.

A waiter came in and glanced interrogatively at Wilson's vis-a-vis, who spoke very slowly and deliberately.

'Bring me a pot of hot tea and a little hot toast,' he said. 'And first be good enough to remove the crust.'

'Very good, sir,' returned the waiter, 'and what's the other gentleman going to have?'

The other glanced at Wilson with a shy and deprecatory smile.

'The other gentleman,' he said, 'must speak for himself.'

'No, sir, I don't mean this gentleman, but the one who came in with you.'

'Nobody came in with me. I am entirely by myself.'

The waiter looked puzzled and lowered his head. When he spoke his tone expressed disbelief.

'Very good, sir. My mistake. Tea and toast, sir.'

'I think I'll have the same,' Wilson interpolated.

The waiter went, leaving behind him that quality of silence which demands to be broken.

'I suppose it's still pretty foggy?' Wilson asked quite superfluously.

'Yes, but it's beginning to move. There's a breath of air sprung up. I don't think it will last much longer.'

'Good!' said Wilson. 'Then perhaps I shall be able to get back to-night.'

'Come far?'

'London. It was quite clear when I started. You've been disappointed too, I suppose?'

The older man nodded.

'Yes, but I haven't come so far for a bad egg. I live only about a mile away. Often see you out with the hounds. You know many people around here?'

'No. Only by sight.' Wilson hesitated and laughed, 'I'm an interloper, you see, and I can hardly expect to make friends in a district where I'm unknown. '

The other looked at him closely and thoughtfully and then nodded slowly.

'My name's Garshaw,' he said, suddenly and unexpectedly.

Wilson inclined his head. 'Mine's Wilson,' he said.

For some reason best known to himself Garshaw seemed immediately to accept Wilson as a friend in whom confidences could be reposed.

'Well, Mr Wilson,' he said, 'I've seen you out with us often enough to feel that I know you quite well.'

'And I you,' said Wilson, 'I don't think you and your friend have missed a meet when I've been out.'

Garshaw stared at him sharply.

'My friend?' he repeated. 'Whom do you mean?'

'The man who always rides with you.'

There was a moment's silence. Then Garshaw spoke very quietly.

'You're mistaken,' he said, i haven't got a friend. What was this man like?'

Wilson tried hard to think. He was perfectly sure that he had seen another man always in close attendance on Garshaw, but he found himself quite incapable of describing him.

'It's funny,' he said, laughing at himself, 'but I couldn't tell you what he's like. I only carry in my mind something which artists would call a post-impression, and it's quite impossible to convey it to you.'

Garshaw smiled faintly.

'It must be your imagination,' he said. 'Like the waiter just now. He thought I had come in with somebody else, and he didn't quite believe it when I told him I hadn't. No, I don't suppose you've so much as seen me exchange a word with anybody. I was going to warn you that you'll find it hard to make friends around here, Mr Wilson. They're a very queer set of people. I say They and not We, because I'm no longer of them.'

Wilson felt embarrassed and naturally wondered what Garshaw had done to erect the hackles of his neighbours. But he could not ask, and merely said:

'Yes, I rather gathered that they were sticky.'

'No-o,' said Garshaw, 'it isn't quite stickiness. I've had my present house for ten years. I'd been out East all my life, and I came home and married a lady fairly well known in the county. All our neighbours were very friendly and hospitable, and continued to be so until my wife died eighteen months ago. Then everything changed, and I'm damned if I know why. People dropped me like a hot coal after she died. I used to be on dining terms with my neighbours and now I'm hardly on nodding terms. And I haven't the least idea what I'm supposed to have done wrong.'

He uttered a baffled laugh which seemed to invite an echo from Wilson.

'Can't you ask?' Wilson suggested.

'My dear sir, how can I? If people choose to treat me off-handedly they must please themselves. And it isn't only the—the gentry. The labourers and village tradespeople shrink away from me and show me pretty plainly that they want to have as little as possible to do with me. It's just an insoluble mystery to me. For over a year now I've been racking my brains trying to think what they can possibly have up against me, and I can't get an inkling of what it is.'

He paused and looked at Wilson anxiously and with a kind of pathos, is there anything about me,' he asked, 'which makes you want to shrink from me? It would be a mistaken kindness if you said No and meant Yes. We're strangers, so you can afford to be frank.'

'No,' said Wilson laughing. 'I hope I seem as agreeable to you as you do to me.'

Garshaw shrugged his shoulders.

'Then why—why is it? I've not done anybody any harm that I know of. I've done nothing that could possibly start the tongue of Scandal wagging. I don't want to seem a hypocrite, but my life has been comparatively blameless, and especially so since I settled here. But I can't even get indoor servants. My groom-gardener and his wife have stuck to me, but they sleep in the cottage. She comes in and gets my meals but she seems to hate doing it. It's as if I were carrying plague germs about with me. The thing's got on my mind, or I shouldn't be telling you about it.'

It occurred very naturally to Wilson that Garshaw, while seeming quite frank, was yet keeping something up his sleeve. He suspected at first that Garshaw had sinned unforgivably against the social or moral code—or knew himself to be suspected of doing so—and preferred not to unbosom himself entirely. At the same time he was sorry for the man and felt attracted to him.

'Why don't you clear out?' he asked.

'Yes—and tacitly plead guilty to whatever I'm supposed to have done. No, Mr Wilson, I never ran away from anything in my life, and I'll stand my ground now. By putting myself in your place I can guess quite well which way your suspicions are tending. I told you I lost my wife eighteen months ago. There is no dispute as to how she met her death. It was an ordinary and natural death—that of pneumonia following upon an attack of influenza. The one thing that I know I am not suspected of is foul play nor could the longest stretch of imagination devise a motive. My wife and I were an ideally happy couple—at least, until her mind began to give way a few months before her death. Then she began to have delusions, Mr Wilson, and to blame me because I could not share them.

'It's the old story. She began to take an interest in psychic matters and soon became absorbed in them. She indulged in that form of self-deception, as I prefer to consider it, which is called Automatic Writing. After a little she had no time or thought for anything else and shocked me deeply by declaring that she had a personal demon, or "familiar", which never left her. I tried to reason with her in vain, and my declining to believe any such nonsense was the cause of the first breach between us. She was not in her own mind when she died, and her last words expressed the dreadful wish that the fiend which had been in attendance on her would transfer his allegiance to me.'

He paused, and Wilson felt called upon to mutter something sympathetic.

There was a certain grim humour in Garshaw's next remark.

'I almost wish that the fiend existed and had taken her at her word. At least I shouldn't have been so lonely.'

Wilson was sorry for the man. He was not devoid of imagination nor of an elementary knowledge of psychology. He knew that these confidences reposed in himself, a stranger, were the result of the unfortunate man's pent-up longing to unbosom himself to somebody. There is nothing in the world quite so lonely as a lonely man or woman with a grievance, and although Jerry Wilson had little doubt but that Garshaw had been ostracized for some very definite reason, he now believed the unfortunate man to be ignorant of the cause and innocent of any wrong intention.

So they took tea together and Jerry Wilson proved a good listener. He heard all about how the Marshes from Brinkchurch, once the closest friends of the Garshaws, were now known to make long detours to avoid meeting the man in 'Coventry'; and how last year Lady Pillidge had, for the first time in ten years, refrained from asking Mr Garshaw to take charge of the coconut shy at her annual fete. These and other similar examples of Mr Garshaw's ostracism were poured into Jerry Wilson's not unsympathetic ears.

'Are you going to dine here?' Garshaw asked at last.

'Yes, I think so. There is no necessity for me to hurry back to Town, so I think I shall stay the night. It depends on how the fog's getting on.'

He went to the window, drew back the curtains and looked out.

'It's almost gone,' he announced, i think I shall go back.'

Garshaw turned in his chair and regarded him almost plaintively.

'No, don't,' he begged. 'The railway services won't have settled down, and you'll have a most uncomfortable journey. Stay here to dinner as my guest, and then let me put you up for the night. We shall be alone in the house, but I promise I can make you quite comfortable, and you can have your early morning tea whenever you like, for Mrs Nelson rises with the lark and comes round to the house before the other birds are awake.'

Jerry Wilson did not particularly want to accept the invitation, but he was sorry for Garshaw, and saw how desperately anxious the poor man was for his company. So it ended in his accepting the invitation with thanks, and looking forward to his visit with a certain amount of curiosity.

What happened afterwards, between then and nine o'clock, seems to be of no particular interest, for Jerry Wilson passes it over with scarcely a word Apparently they dined at about eight, and at nine o'clock they set out to walk to Garshaw's house a mile outside the village.

The fog was all gone now and a moon was rising. The night promised to be fine and clear. The two men asked each other idly why the Clerk of the Weather couldn't have arranged the climatic conditions a little differently, and bemoaned the lost day's hunting.

Garshaw lived in a good-sized, well-planned modern house which stood in about two acres of garden. Before entering the house Garshaw conducted his guest round to the garden at the back, which was separated from open fields by iron railings about four feet high. Out in the fields Jerry Wilson could see the dim shapes of cattle.

'I bet one of those damned bullocks has been in the garden,' Garshaw said. 'They're always getting in, although I never catch 'em. But how they get in and out again baffles my man Nelson and me. Yes! Come and look here!'

He pointed to a large round flower-bed, and Wilson, following him, saw quite distinctly the prints of cloven hoofs. Garshaw swore under his breath and smoothed the soft earth with the sole of his shoe.

'Now,' he said, 'look at those railings. Do you see a gap anywhere? I don't. And can a cow or a bullock jump railings as high as that?'

'Horned cattle can jump better than most people think,' Wilson replied, 'although they're too lazy to do it often. I remember the trouble we had when I was a boy, keeping cows off a roped-in village cricket pitch. They used to invade it out of sheer cussedness, or because the watered grass was finer and greener than the pasture they were feeding from. '

'Well,' said Garshaw grimly, 'if I catch any cattle in my garden I'll shoot 'em. Then I don't know what'll happen, because I'm not on the best of terms with my neighbours as it is. Now let's go in. I think I can offer you a really good cigar.'

They sat up smoking and talking until after eleven, when a move was made for bed. The windows of the room allotted to Jerry Wilson looked out on to the garden behind the house and the pastures beyond. The room was well furnished and restful, and the bed comfortable. He was sound asleep within a few minutes of lying down.

He woke between one and two—it was two minutes short of the half hour, according to his watch. He lay awake wondering what had roused him, and conscious that it must have been some sound. Further cogitation convinced him that it must have proceeded from the garden, and, remembering what Garshaw had said about the marauding cattle, he jumped out of bed and went to the window.

He was just too late to see something. Whatever was moving in the garden was coming towards the house and flashed out of his line of vision as he looked out. He stood staring and listening intently, and thought he heard a stealthy sound from the door at the back of the hall.

Jerry Wilson was not a coward. He was certainly the last man in the world to be afraid of burglars; but he owns quite frankly that a sort of horror took hold on him so that he could do nothing for a minute or two but stand and listen.

Then the stairs began to creak, and the sound of creaking grew nearer.

Somebody or something shuffled almost silently down the landing, past Jerry Wilson's door, and the sounds died out at the door of Garshaw's room.

Jerry Wilson stood hesitating for a long minute. Then he managed to rouse himself. For all he knew to the contrary somebody had broken into the house and his host might be in danger. So, hating with all his heart the task he had imposed upon himself, he crept down the landing to Garshaw's door.

He tapped and received no answer, and called Garshaw by name with the same lack of result. Then, softly, he pushed open the door and looked inside. The moon was still up and there was plenty of light. He could see the bed quite clearly, and the mound of bedclothes which marked where Garshaw lay asleep. Garshaw was plainly asleep, breathing deeply and regularly, and but for him the room was empty to the eye.

To the eye, yes, but not to the ear. Wilson held his own breath to make quite sure, and then, to his unutterable horror he was aware that two people—one of them invisible—were drawing breath inside that room. He was never able to say how he controlled his nerve sufficiently to close the door so quietly as not to rouse Garshaw, but he owns to having rushed back to his own room as if all the fiends in the Pit were at his heels. What he suspected then he didn't say, but one can be sure that he remembered without much comfort Garshaw's account of the last words of his late wife. Daylight puts a very different complexion on the terrors of darkness, and when Jerry Wilson woke with the sun streaming in upon him he was able half to persuade himself that he had been the victim of nightmare or a too lively imagination. After Mrs Nelson had brought him his early tea, he rose, bathed, dressed and went downstairs into the garden.

At least one of the horned beasts grazing in the pastures beyond had invaded the garden during the night. It had left unmistakable traces on another flower-bed. In the kitchen garden on his left an old man with a red, dried-up face was cutting cabbages. Doubtless, he thought, this was Nelson, the groom-gardener. Wilson went over to chat with him. The old man gave him a strange look and a stranger greeting.

' 'Mornin, sir? You the gentleman that's been stayin' the night? I 'ope you slept comfortable. You're the first gentleman bar the master that's slept in that house for above a bit.'

'Really?' said Wilson, 'I understood that Mr Garshaw was rather lonely.'

The old man spat.

'Lonely! Gar! He ain't lonely, and won't be while he's got his friend.'

'What friend?'

'The one what's always about with him—the one as nobody likes the look of! Ah, he's a queer one, he is, and he ain't no good. That's why Master's lost all 'is other friends—they can't stand the looks of that new mate of his. Nobody knows who he is or where he comes from, but we all knows as 'e's a bad 'un!'

Jerry Wilson felt the roots of his hair pricking his scalp. He made an effort to change the subject.

'Some more cattle got into the garden last night,' he said.

Old Nelson eyed him queerly.

'Was there!' he said. 'Oh, was there? And what kind o' cattle could get over yon railings? The cow that jumped over the moon, I shouldn't wonder.'

'Well, there are the traces,' said Wilson with a half laugh.

The old man showed signs of stirring himself.

'Show me, sir,' he said, 'I've seen 'em before, mind, but I'd like to see these new ones.'

'Come on, then,' said Wilson, and led the way over.

The old man grinned cynically at the prints plainly visible upon the surface of the bed.

'And what kind of cow or steer ever left marks like that, sir?' he asked.

'There's the cleft, I grant you, but apart from that, did you ever see cattle with long hoofs shaped like a man's feet? Because I never did, and I've been with horned cattle and horses all my life.'

'It was then that Jerry Wilson's soul turned sick within him, and mingled with that nausea was a sudden and deep pity for Garshaw.

'Poor devil!' he thought, 'poor devil! And he doesn't know. He doesn't know!'

Garshaw was found dead in bed a few months later. He had died in his sleep of haemorrhage of the brain. There was evidence that just prior to his death he had risen in the night to drive cattle out of his garden.

At least his naked footprints were found, pointing away from the house, side by side with the cloven hoof-prints of some horned beast.

The Cottage in the Wood

The doctor understood her type very well. 'Mutton dressed as lamb' it used to be called. Middle age trying to masquerade as girlhood. One of the better class type of unfortunates— that even these should be classed and graded!—who tried to sell her spurious youth to the unwary. Had been a
gentlewoman too, poor devil. And now she had danced the Dance of Death almost to the last step.

He had turned away and stood preoccupied in the simple act of setting his stethoscope down upon a small table. A voice spoke from the couch behind him, a voice which shook in its effort to sound casual.

'Well?' it said.

He turned. Madge Ridley was sitting up. She looked into his face but saw only his professional mask.

'Yes,' he said, 'you've been overdoing it, you know. You can't dance'—he eyed her teadily—'and drink—all night and every night for ever.

Nobody's heart could stand that sort of thing indefinitely. I'm going to give you a prescription for a tonic, and then I want you to promise me to go away quietly somewhere and rest.'

'Into the country?'

'That would be advisable.'

'Am I—really ill?'

'You are worn out. You need rest.'

'Shall I see a specialist?'

'My dear madam, he can only tell you what I have told you. Why waste two guineas?'

Yes, why send her to a specialist, when a student could have blurted out the truth to her? How long had she? Three months? Three months at the very most; probably much less.

'Shall I get better?' Madge Ridley asked, again with that effort to control her voice.

He lied. Why frighten her?

'That depends entirely on yourself,' he said coldly. 'Remember that no doctor can make you better.'

'Thank you. I understand. Thank you very much.'

Within another minute she had paid him and was gone, walking very slowly and leaving behind her a trail of perfume at which the doctor sniffed contemptuously. The post-War type of man-snatcher! And she ought to have had a man of her own and a happy home and a family growing up around her.

'I wonder what her story is,' he thought.

And then his manservant came in to announce another patient, and he forgot her.

Those who remember that there is nothing new under the sun will not expect to be startled by too much originality in the tale of Madge Ridley's life.

She was an orphan, and owed everything she had to a genteel aunt who lived in a small house on Campden Hill, where she took up her abode as soon as she left school. The means of the genteel aunt were slender, but she was too genteel to dream of allowing Madge to do anything towards earning her own living. That, of course, was before the War. This budding rose, the aunt reflected, would soon be gathered by some Mr Right who came from somewhere south or west of Notting Hill.

As it happened it was the son of a poor country rector who first inspired and returned Madge Ridley's love. He rescued Madge's dog from the jaws of a larger dog and insisted on carrying him home for her. Such incidents used to be called romantic.

Larry Prevost lived in a boarding-house in Notting Hill, convenient to the Central London Railway which carried him every weekday to a wretchedly underpaid job in a City office. He was a nice-looking fresh-faced boy with crisp fair hair which always curled, no matter how closely he kept it cropped. He was a lance-corporal in a London Territorial battalion and for Madge's sake he neglected his drills, just as for her sake he starved himself of lunches to buy her flowers and chocolates.

The aunt received this wolf in sheep's clothing into her house, without the least idea that a love affair was pending; and having unwittingly done all she could to encourage it, was furious when the truth came out.

She owned that Larry was a nice boy and a gentleman, but years must elapse before he could afford to marry—if ever at all. The young couple denied this, and expressed their willingness to settle down in a nice cosy attic and live on bread and cheese—from which it will not be hard for the discerning to guess their approximate ages. Storms rocked the little house for at least six weeks. Madge, who knew how to weep violently, vowed repeatedly that she would never, never marry anyone but Larry.

Eventually the aunt, whose heart was as soft as her poor old head, gave way and permitted what she called an 'understanding'.

So this poor little romance—which belonged to Fairyland and had no place in London Town—began its short sweet life. It was too frail and fragile a thing ever to live; one knew instinctively that some clumsy, careless foot would crush it into the dust. It nearly died in the beginning, for Larry went down with pneumonia, and for weeks Madge wandered like a little pale ghost between her home and the hospital where he lay.

He recovered. The doctors dragged him up from the Valley of the Shadow, and at each stage of his recovery Madge knew the gradual alleviation of a pain which had once seemed insupportable. During his convalescence she enjoyed the happiest time of her life.

He went to stay with his parents in the Surrey rectory on the edge of Bladleigh Woods. Madge was invited to keep him company. That was how she spent three weeks with her lover in Fairyland.

It was high midsummer, a time of long cloudless days; and Larry's instructions were to keep in the open air and be as lazy as he liked. The memory of those days always returned to Madge as one long cool dream of pine-woods where it was always twilight, of wandering hand in hand, and sudden embraces when the sweetness of them almost hurt. What talks they had about the future!—for they were young enough to believe themselves captains of their destinies, and looked forward smiling into a roseate dawn. Fate at her loom smiled cynically and went on with her harsh, interminable task. Austria was reaching for the throat of Servia, and Death's agents were already busy in the munition factories of the world.

They played games too—childish games—but Larry was not allowed strenuous exercise, and here Blick, who always accompanied them, made himself useful.

Blick was Larry's fox-terrier, a dog of almost super-canine intelligence. He specialized in games of hide and seek. Madge would hide among the trees and Larry would send Blick to find her. He always succeeded, and by tugging at her skirt and running before her, invariably brought her back to his master.

There was a keeper's cottage in the wood, empty now that the land had been given to the nation. And because the cottage properly belonged to a fairy-tale—surely it was the very one in which Hop-o'-my-thumb was born—they decided that they must live in it after they were married. Then Larry was to give up going to the horrible office, and write stories—for everybody knows that story-writing is the laziest, happiest and easiest way of earning a living, once you know how to do it. So they were to live happy ever after in Bladleigh Woods in the scent of the pines and their voices in the wind for perpetual music.

Larry did not go out with his battalion at the outbreak of war. It was too soon after his illness. But he went out with the first draft. Madge saw him off. That was the most terrible recollection of her life. Victoria Station in the dark, small hours of a bleak autumn morning. The hollow tramp of men marching up the platform. 'It's a long way to Tipperary, it's a long way to go. Halt! Right turn! Men climbing into compartments, eight in each. Some confusion while packs and rifles were being hoisted on to the racks. Men trying to smile, women trying not to weep. The pathetic figure of a young girl handing sprigs of white heather to the poor doomed boys. And the chill of the raw, dark morning striking into the bones and accentuating the tragic hopelessness of it all.

Tragic, desperate last embraces. Stand back, please—and a slamming of doors. Brown faces looking out, still smiling, and a waving of hands. The train gliding out, and women unaffectedly sobbing now. Hands and faces still visible for a little while, and then even the rear red light of the train being lost in the darkness. The little girl with the white heather—God knows who she was—being led away. Breakfast? Coffee? Oh, what did anything matter now?

The world was shattered as completely as if the Last Trump had sounded. This was the setting of Madge's last memory of Larry Prevost. She knew then and there that he had gone to his death; so that when the news came two months later it was scarcely a shock to her.

But if it were scarcely a shock it uprooted and destroyed something that had grown into the very core of her being. She ceased to believe in God. While Larry lived she could believe in Him and pray to Him. What did it matter to her that thousands of other young men were being slaughtered? Now Larry was dead there was no God. She lost both at the same blow. Twice she had endured the agony of Larry's death, and once he had been given back to her, only to be finally snatched from her again. God—if He existed—had played with her, deliberately torturing her.

She had expended all her emotions, and the source from which they sprang had run dry. Nothing mattered now. She became a flesh-and-blood machine, a breathing automaton to whom hope and despair, joy and sorrow, love and hate, were words as meaningless to her as if they belonged to a language which she had never learned.

Of course she got a job. It was fashionable in those days for young women to go to work, and the genteel aunt no longer tried to dissuade her. She became a clerk in a Government department and earned her own bread and butter. There was a colonel who had been invalided home and who was sorry for her and petted her. He was one of those many middle-aged gentlemen who have, in moments of expansion, pathetic tales of matrimonial infelicity to unfold. Madge understood him so much better than his wife! He made a habit of taking her out to dinner, and she learned that, although wine may be a mocker, it appears first of all in the guise of a very sincere comforter. Before the gallant colonel returned home and gave his lawful wife another opportunity of understanding him the affair had progressed some little way beyond platonics.

The colonel had many successors. Madge Ridley had to find them, for she had developed a taste for expensive living. What did anything matter now? Besides which, the aunt, having invested nearly every penny in Russian stock, died under the blow delivered at more exalted heads by Messrs Lenin and Trotsky. Madge Ridley found herself with an earning capacity of about five pounds a week, an illimitable capacity for spending and a gift for making herself attractive to men.

Up to this point there is nothing remarkable or unusual in the story of her life.

Madge Ridley took the doctor's advice seriously. If she did not particularly want to live she clung to the natural habit of living. No swimmer has ever been able to drown himself by the mere act of jumping into the water. There was still just enough left in life to make it worthwhile to go on drawing breath after breath. If there were no God, no Larry, no future state, at least there were wine and good food, bright lights, dancing, music, admiration.

She had a little money and some jewellery on which more could be raised. She could keep herself modestly for many months before feeling the authentic pinch of poverty. But she hated the country. Besides, she suspected that, isolated from her friends and driven back upon her own resources, she would begin to think. Not for years had she dared to think.

She was a London sparrow, strangely untravelled even in England. She had never spent more than three or four consecutive nights outside London except at Bladleigh, during those happy weeks when Larry was convalescent. Perhaps that was why she chose Bladleigh. Because she had once been happy there it seemed the least undesirable country place in which to bury herself alive. She remembered the peace of it and the healing smell of the pines. Larry's father was dead, and nobody in the village was likely to remember her or, at worst, to recognize her.

'I'll try it,' she thought, 'and if I can't stand it I can come back.'

Madge remembered a Mrs Upcott who used to let lodgings in Bladleigh. Mr Upcott was an insurance agent, compelled to toil among those who were blind or indifferent to the benefits which the Hand and Heart Mutual was willing to shower on their heads in exchange for a few pence a week.

Strangely enough, Mr and Mrs Upcott were still there, living behind the same brass plate, and Mrs Upcott had not altered by the length or tint of a grey hair since Madge had last seen her. The depression in local insurance seemed to have been maintained ever since Madge's previous visit, and Mrs Upcott leapt at the chance of letting two of her rooms.

Madge called herself Mrs James, and might have called herself by her real name, for Mrs Upcott had no recollection of the young lady who was going to marry Mr Larry and had come to stay at the Rectory all those years ago. The lodger ate an improvised supper and announced her intention of going out for a quiet walk before bedtime.

Bladleigh had changed, marching abreast with the great world outside.

The Bungalow Fiend had been at work, and smallholders were busy in the act of committing financial suicide with pigs and poultry. Council houses of the approved design had been erected where they were best calculated to offend the eye. The old village inn had been pulled down and in its place had grown a red brick horror with, however, accommodation to deserve the official blessings of the A.A. and the R.A.C. But the church, symbol of eternity, remained unchanged, and the Crusader, long since unprayed-for, still slept in effigy on his tomb.

Madge hesitated by the church door and nearly entered. She knew just what she would see. She remembered in detail every picture in stained-glass visible from the Rectory pew. Sunny Sunday morning and motes dancing in long beams of light. Strange how it all came back— with the smell of moth-ball from the villagers' best clothes. And Somebody sitting beside her who nudged her slyly when his father, droning in the pulpit, halted suddenly to grope for a word. She was beyond feeling, beyond caring, and she could look down the long road of memory with undimmed eyes, but she was strangely unwilling to re-enter the church. She passed on, wondering why.

She found herself on the edge of the pine woods. It was already growing dusk, and to walk among the trees was like stepping out of evening into night. But there a deep peace abode, and sounds were hushed, all but the whisper of the trees which was like the voice of the sea on a calm day. And there was that fresh, green, unforgettable smell which brought the Past upon her as an horizon, seen through glasses, leaps at the beholder.

Somewhere over yonder, in the direction she was facing, was the empty cottage. But no, she would not go in that direction. There was no need. But she and Larry had talked about that cottage the last time she was in the wood: how they were going to furnish. . . .

She and Larry! She stopped suddenly and wondered, wild-eyed, catching at a straw of hope. There was the wood, cool and fragrant and unchanged.

How long since she had last walked in it? Fifteen years ago, or was it only yesterday? Fifteen years! Impossible—oh, impossible. And was Larry dead, and she a dying wanton? It was incredible. It simply wasn't true. She had fancied it all in one morbid moment. She would find Larry in a minute, and Larry would hold her close and kiss her and tell her what a little idiot she was!

She toyed with the thought, even as the poor doomed king plotted unlikely wonders. Those gentle footfalls on the soft pine needles—surely that was Larry stealing up to take her by surprise. But no, they were merely the echo of her own tread; they stopped when she stopped. Then Reality burst savagely upon her, shouldering Fancy on one side. In one blinding flash of light, kindled by some spark from the brain, she saw her own naked soul. She saw what she had let life make of her and what she had let life steal from her. God lost, Larry lost, all lost!

But with the lightning came the rain. The springs which had been dry for years began to run. Suddenly her cheeks were wet with the first tears which had sprung from her eyes since the day Larry went away. It was as if all in her nature that was sweet and true and pure had escaped from her to hide in the wood and had awaited her coming throughout the years. And, as the tears fell, she felt the very near presence of Larry, and cried out wildly to him by name.

'Larry! Larry! I know you're somewhere near. Come to me! Help me!

Save me! It's Madge . . . little Madge. Oh, God, don't keep him from me? Oh, God, have mercy. . . .'

She sank on to her knees, clutched at the bole of a pine tree, and pressed her forehead against the rough bark.

'Oh, God, I know Larry lives. I didn't believe it for years but I know it now. Don't keep us apart in the hereafter. I've been a wicked woman, but punish me some other way. I couldn't bear the burden You laid upon me. You gave him back to me once when I thought I had lost him, and I couldn't bear it the second time.'

She clung fast to the tree as if it were some symbol of faith.

'Oh, Christ, you saved Mary Magdalen—save me. I can't undo what I have done, nor unlive the life I have lived. But if there is redemption through suffering, let my suffering count. I know I am soon going to die. That doctor knew, although he wouldn't tell me. I've so little time in which to make amends. What can I do but cry for mercy? Don't keep me apart from Larry through all eternity. I couldn't help myself. I couldn't bear my life. I'

She choked suddenly and then her voice came steadfastly.

'I can't make excuses for myself. I am only weak, and a sinner. I can say nothing in my defence, I am sorry . . . sorry . . . sorry. . . . Have mercy . . .have mercy. . . .'

And after Madge Ridley had poured out her heart in words a deep peace came upon her, although her eyes were still streaming when she looked up. It was then that the extraordinary experience befell her.

Through the blur of tears she saw something small and white running towards her through a maze of trees. She stared at it in amazement, for there was no doubt at all that it was a little white dog, and it reminded her of Blick. It was just like Blick as he used to run and find her and lead her back to his master.

A few moments later the little dog had uttered a short triumphant bark and leaped upon her, squirming as if he expected to be petted and made much of. And Madge uttered a short cry and stood up.

'It is you, Blick! Oh, Blick, darling! But no, it can't be. You must have been dead for years and years! Little dogs don't live very long, do they, Blick? I wonder if you missed your master. Not so much as'

But Blick—yes, surely it was Blick—tugged at her skirt and ran before her barking, just as he had done in the old days. She followed him dazedly, half fearfully, not quite daring to hope. He trotted before her through the trees, and kept returning to make sure that she was following, as he had always done.

Under a pine sat Larry in his old grey flannel coat, idly whittling a piece of wood with his pocket knife. He looked up at her and smiled.

'Hullo,' he remarked, 'where have you been? It's taken Blick an awful long time to find you.'

The tears were running down her cheeks.

'Oh, Larry,' she cried, 'such a long time! Such a long time!'

He stared at her in chagrin, rose and slipped his arms around her.

'Madge! Madge, darling! What's the matter? Crying on your wedding-day! Surely that's not lucky!'

'Wedding-day! Larry, don't you understand? Everything's gone wrong.

I'm dreaming. You're dreaming, too, perhaps. But, Larry darling, you're dead, you know.'

He kissed her fondly.

'Well, that's not bad for a dead man, anyway,' he laughed. 'What is the matter with you, Madge? Matrimony can't have turned your brain already. When and how did I happen to die?'

'You were killed in the War,' she sobbed.

'The War? The Boer War, you mean? Let me see, how old was I when that was on?'

'Oh, Larry, don't you understand? The war with Germany.'

He laughed again.

'First I've heard of it. I suppose there will be war with Germany someday, and then we'll show them what the Terriers can do. Now I tell you what it is. You've been asleep and dreaming things.' He wagged a reproving finger at her. 'What ought I to say to a girl who strays away from her husband within a few hours of getting married and falls asleep under a tree?'

She uttered a deep sigh.

'Larry, were we . . . Yes, I'm beginning to remember. And we're going to live in the cottage, aren't we?'

New memories had crept across the background of the old, like slides thrust across the face of a lantern.

'Well, considering you chose the furniture!' he laughed.

So she had. That was funny! And she had undoubtedly married Larry that morning. Her mind was a tangle in which the real and the unreal were inextricably mingled. She kissed him and clung fast to him.

'Oh, Larry! So it was only a dream after all! Make me sure! Make me sure! I dreamed horrible things not only about you but about myself.'

He made her sure in the way known to lovers.

'You must never dream horrible things again,' he whispered.

'I won't,' she whispered back. 'Hold me very tight, Larry.   Keep very near me always. Larry, darling, I'm so happy . . . now.'

He bent and kissed her again.

'And I too. Come home, Madge . . . my wife.'

'Yes, take me home,' she breathed.

So, linked by the arms and with Blick running before them, they walked slowly through the wood towards where the lights of the cottage shone out between the trees.

Madge Ridley was found in the morning kneeling by a tree, her arms clasping the whole and her face pressed against the bark. She was quite dead as we understand death. There were traces of tears about her eyes but her lips were smiling.

The Strange Case of Dolly Frewan

Chertford is one of those Thames-side towns which are so easily accessible from London that they might fairly be called suburbs. The larger houses are mostly inhabited by a section of the community vaguely described as 'river people'. The men, nearly all of whom make a daily journey to offices in the City, spend most of their summer weekends on the river, and their womenfolk—or such of them as can spare the time—almost live on the water between the months of April and September. Taking them on the whole they are a cheerful, vulgar, respectable, brainless set of people.

Old Philip Lockland inhabited one of the biggest houses overlooking the river. Between his garden gate and the water's edge was a breadth of metalled road and a thin strip of shrubbery, known as the Promenade or the Public Gardens, which flanked the south bank of the river for about a quarter of a mile. On the opposite bank was the towpath and the grounds of a private estate which had not yet been divided into eligible building sites.

Old Lockland was an outside broker who lived very expensively and always in a state of feverish anxiety. He had a fat over-dressed wife whose mental life was spent on the brinks of her husband's volcanoes, a daughter safely married to some spatted nonentity in Surbiton, and a son aged twenty-one, who accompanied him daily to the office. The boy's name was Reggie.

All the young men of Chertford are either Douglases, Reggies, Percies, or Berties. Young Reggie shared his father's railway compartment going to and returning from the City, occupied a stool within range of the parental vision, and lived at home on an illiberal allowance of pocket-money. He had never been permitted much liberty, nor had he been given any opportunity to learn self-reliance, and he was unwholesomely afraid of his father.

A strict disciplinarian was old Lockland, and although his reputation in the City was not too good, nor was his name received with enthusiasm in orphanages or among widowed ladies, he was a stem moralist in private life.

The boy, who was weak and rather stupid, would have died sooner than bring himself to face his father and confess a peccadillo. While it scared him to speculate on what the old man might say if he knew what the younger generation of the town already knew, it amused him to reflect that he was not the docile and decorous youth that his father imagined him to be. He was wont to boast, after the manner of his kind and age, that he 'lived his life'.

The average half-baked youngster, tied to an uncongenial home-life, but given the after-dinner liberty of the streets, is fairly sure to get into more or less serious mischief. Chertford abounded in young clerks of about Reggie's own age, who prowled about in the evenings from one hotel to another, where barmaids with good looks and loose tongues were admitted attractions. They spoke in tones of exaggerated refinement, and took great pains to cultivate a style of speech—dashing and yet rather bored—which they vaguely connected with Oxford. They learned all the new slang before it was nine months old, talked learnedly of racing, and risked occasional shillings, which always became pounds in the course of airy conversation. Whenever they could afford it they got drunk to prove that they were not only gentlemen but gentlemen of spirit. Many a time Reggie crept up to bed wondering bemusedly if his father or mother would 'notice anything' if either happened to meet him.

Thus Reggie spent his evenings in an atmosphere of beer, gambling, smutty stories and pitiful affectations. But sometimes he and a chosen companion would prowl the streets in the hope of 'getting off with a couple of girls. There were two large drapers' shops in Chertford, whose staffs provided Reggie and his friends with most of their amorous adventures. These girls roamed the streets after the day's work, generally in pairs, and most of them were willing to throw a smile in exchange for a masculine cough, to halt and say 'Good evening', to play their part in the conventional farce that they had previously been introduced, and afterwards to be escorted along the deserted towing path or to some seat in a dusky lane.

To do them justice, the behaviour of the young men was not generally so scandalous as they afterwards made it out to be. There was kissing and telling, but a great deal more telling than kissing. Innocence was not a virtue highly esteemed among the unlicked cubs of Chertford.

Reggie L.ockland met Dolly Frewan for the first time on a mild February evening. He was with young Huntman and she with a friend whom she called Olive. There was a change of partners and then a walk by the river. Reggie Lockland paired off with Dolly.

Dolly Frewan was a coarse type of brunette, but not ill-looking, a recruit at Humphries and Howe's, and a stranger to the district. She mouthed her vowels with self-conscious refinement, and told him how her father was a gentleman who had lost his money, and how she didn't ought to have been in a shop. However, she was flattered by the attentions of a son of one of the great big houses by the river.

Afterwards he met her by appointment on one or two evenings every week, and soon found that she had more to give than most of the more cautious of her kind. He was able to boast truthfully now, where hitherto he had been reduced to lying. Better still, he was believed by the cognoscenti, for he was not Dolly's only male friend.

He had known her just a little more than two months when the tragedy happened. On a certain April evening they had made an appointment to meet at half-past eight on the town side of Chertford Bridge. He swallowed down his early dinner at a table overcrowded with silver, between walls over-crowded with pictures in heavy gilt frames, and walked out into freedom. It was a clear mild night of stars and after a day of broad sunshine.

People who were not above using stock phrases had been saying all day that they could feel spring in the air. Many pleased suburbanites alleged that they had heard the cuckoo. Certainly summer was on the march, and the first swift scouts had already arrived. Reggie went out feeling that despite his parents and the office and one or two pressing and secret debts the world was quite worth living in after all.

The way to the place of assignation took him past the George, which was one of the favourite houses of resort. A glance at the illuminated dial of the Town Hall clock assured him that he had time to drink half a pint of bitter.

He stepped inside and was greeted by half a dozen acquaintances. He stayed only five minutes, but it served a purpose yet undreamed of. He had been seen about that night, a circumstance which later put a brake on many tongues wagging in idle speculation. Afterwards he sweated to think how easily he might have told somebody that he was going out with Dolly Frewan. But he had been going out with her so regularly of late that it seemed hardly worthwhile to mention it.

It was dark by the bridge where he met her. They crossed it, meeting no one known to either of them. Details which were not at the time selected by his conscious mind were stored in some secret closet of the memory and were afterwards surprisingly revealed to him. He remembered quite clearly the half-dozen pedestrians whom they met while crossing the bridge, none of whom gave them so much as a casual glance. Once on the towing-path they were alone with the river and the night breeze.... They sat side by side on some steps where boating-parties land.

To-night Dolly Frewan seemed not to be herself; she was preoccupied and unresponsive. He kept asking her what was the matter, and when at last she told him she stunned him for the moment as completely as if the words had been so many heavy blows of a bludgeon.

At first he did not believe her. He had heard of fellows being 'had' like that before. And after all why should it be he? He wasn't the only one. . . .

But her vehemence shouted down all doubt, every objection. She seemed frightened, and in her fear she was masterful, shrill, vindictive.

'What are we to do?' he asked helplessly at last, still unable to grasp the full meaning of the frankest statement a woman can make to a man.

'Do?' She was impatient with him, angry, as if none of the blame were hers. 'You got me into this mess, so you can get me out of it.

'Tisn't as if there wasn't time for us to get married.'

Married! How could he marry in secret on his paltry little allowance?

More impossible still, the thought of telling his father. His fear of the tyrant grew and grew monstrously with every second. He began to stammer, to mutter half intelligibly. She had the advantage of clearer speech and a higher pitch of voice.

'My dad's a gentleman, too. Yours'll have to do something for us. Won't be the first time that men have had to give their sons allowances to get married on all of a sudden. You'll have to go and tell him.'

Terror had a stranglehold of him now. It was crushing him, squeezing him like an orange. In his agony all the nerves of action were slipping out of his control. Dolly Frewan saw and triumphed.

'If you don't go and tell him, I shall.'

He sprang up as if she had uttered an instant threat, and caught hold of her as if to stop her from putting it into immediate fulfilment. Really, he didn't know what he was doing. Never afterwards was he vouchsafed a clear memory of that moment.

A column of water rose up and drenched him. Chronologically his memory ever afterwards placed that first, before the harsh cry and the heavy splash. He was standing there alone, and Dolly had vanished even from the sudden turmoil of water at his feet.

There was a strong current after recent spring floods. Some yards downstream he saw a hand grasping and clutching at nothing . . . then a face . . . then only a vague struggling shape below the surface. He ran along the bank towards the spot, crying out in horror. Had he been able to swim he would have jumped in; he was almost sure he would have jumped in. He told himself so afterwards a thousand, thousand times. It was difficult to gauge the pace of the current, and before he could realize it he had lost her.

Dolly Frewan would trouble him no more alive.

He ran back towards the bridge, gasping and sobbing.

'Oh, God, I didn't do it purposely! I'm not a murderer, am I? I didn't, did I? It was all an accident. It was an accident, I'm almost—almost sure. Oh, God, don't let me be hanged! We were struggling and she just slipped. That's how it was.'

But until the moment of his own death he never knew whether his will had countenanced the deed, whether he had merely meant to hold her, or whether an impulse of malice had sent her to her death. Memory, writing the interminable diary of big and little things, sometimes scrawling the little things so illegibly that they can never be re-read, but still always writing—memory had left the tablet of that moment blank.

It is my task to record straight history, and not to draw upon suppositions in an attempt to describe the hell endured by young Reggie Lockland during the next few days. Imagination assembled against him actual witnesses of the event, lynx-eyed prowlers in the darkness who had seen the struggle on the steps. Young men who knew that he was in the habit of going out with Dolly Frewan would come forward and betray him. Dolly herself must surely have told somebody of her appointment that evening. Once cornered and questioned he must lie or tell at least part of the truth. To lie, and to be caught out in that lie, he knew to be fatal. So men were hanged at nearly every Sessions. To admit even part of the truth would mean an interview with his father, which he lacked the moral courage even to imagine.

He lived in a nightmare intensified by a clogging sense of guilt. It was all very well to tell himself that he, Reggie Lockland, could not possibly be a murderer, because he was Reggie Lockland, known to all and sundry—himself included—as a harmless and decent sort of chap, and that he hadn't intended to push Dolly into the river. It did not answer the question which repeated itself in his fevered brain while he was awake or sleeping: 'Did I? Did I?'

And Reggie Lockland was lucky, as the meaning of luck is universally understood. His name was hardly breathed in connection with Dolly Frewan, whose body was found next morning below Chertford Weir. It was taken to a mortuary close at hand, where a local doctor made a cursory post-mortem and an inquest followed.

The inquest was very formal and unexciting. Even the local paper spared it no more than an inch or two of space under the well-worn caption, 'Sad River Fatality'. A friend of the deceased with whom she had lodged said that Dolly was a bright and cheerful girl who seemed to have no troubles. She knew that Dolly was going out that evening, but didn't know where. She was just her normal self when she set out. Parents from North London said that Dolly had no troubles as far as they knew. Pathological evidence followed.

There were no signs of violence, nor was there any apparent reason—the usual reason in these cases—why she should take her own life. Thus Reggie knew that she had either deceived herself or sought to deceive him. The coroner remarked—as if the suicide theory were the only alternative to her having met her death by accident—that there seemed no reason to suppose that she had made away with herself, and suggested that she had probably slipped or stumbled into the river from the towpath. Too many bodies came over Chertford Weir during the boating season for the affair to be considered in any way remarkable. A bored jury, with a profound distaste for the duties of citizenship imposed on it, brought in a verdict of 'Found Drowned', there being no evidence to show how the deceased had come to be in the water.

Among the young men of Chertford who knew Dolly Frewan the affair created something of a stir, and occasioned a certain amount of desultory discussion. There was not the least suspicion of foul play. When somebody said, 'It's a wonder Reggie Lockland wasn't with her that night,' somebody else said, 'No, I saw him down at the George.' He had been in the George, although only for five minutes. It was enough to save him from being awkwardly questioned. If there had been the least suspicion and Reggie Lockland had been asked to account for his movements, a very different state of affairs might have been produced. As it was, the word went round among the cubs: 'Don't say anything to poor old Reggie. He looks horribly sick. I believe he was fond of her.'

It does not take the world very long to forget a shopgirl. After a few days Dolly Frewan's name was scarcely ever mentioned. But meanwhile Reggie Lockland had been even sicker than he looked, and two days after the inquest he had a complete breakdown. The family doctor passed him over to a specialist, who ordered him complete rest and change. Even old Lockland succumbed to a suggestion that the boy had been working too hard. He was sent at great expense to a nursing-home on the East Coast, run by a doctor who dealt extensively in cases of nervous collapse. This doctor found Reggie extremely interesting as a patient, but made little of him.

When Reggie Lockland returned home he was very little better. Except in moments of wild and unrestrained imagination he had no longer any fear of his skin. But he suffered from something more than a plain consciousness of guilt; his complex was to suspect himself without being sure, to believe without positively knowing.

He still suffered occasional vague terrors that the truth, as he suspected it, might still come to light. There were people who believed in spiritualism, believed that they could talk to the dead and receive messages from them.

Suppose—just suppose—there might be something in it? Suppose the spirit of Dolly Frewan told her story to some medium, who in turn gave it to the world and started a series of inquiries which might enmesh him even now! He had never heard of such a thing happening, and he did not believe in spiritualism, but his mind kept open house to every hideous self-suggestion. He did not return to the office; he had doctor's orders to rest and keep as much as possible in the fresh air; so he moped at home, with little to distract his mind from a perpetual harking back to a certain April evening. His parents, fearful for his sanity, now let him do exactly as he liked. Instead of repression he now had perfect freedom. He was quick to realize the situation, and soon it was he who bullied them. They suffered him, believing that it would be unsafe to cross him.

About a year after the death of Dolly Frewan, young Reggie Lockland fell in love. Mavis Hope was the daughter of a neighbour who was also 'something in the City'. She was a pretty, fluffy, fair-haired, pink-cheeked little thing, who began by tolerating Reggie out of pity, and ended by forming a genuine attachment to him. The affair had no official sanction, but it was welcomed by both the Locklands and the Hopes.

Reggie Lockland's people hoped that a happy love affair might be the tonic needed to restore Reggie to his old state of health. Obviously there could be no talk of an engagement until his health and working capacity were restored; but meanwhile it was perhaps the best thing that could have happened. The Hopes, on their side, had no objection. There was an even chance that old Lockland, if he avoided prison or bankruptcy, would die a rich man. A formal engagement was of course out of the question until Reggie Lockland had made a complete recovery, but meanwhile there seemed no harm in letting the young things play. It was a fine summer, and the pair spent many hours a day on the river. Between the elder Hopes and the elder Locklands acquaintanceship strengthened to something like friendship.

Mrs Hope was able to offer consolation to Mrs Lockland by assuring her that young people often suffered from 'nerves' and made complete recoveries. There was Mavis, Mavis had caused anxiety some little time ago. She had suffered from strange 'ideas' which were almost—well, almost 'delusions'.

She used to think that spirits other than her own were trying to get possession of her body, and used to fear going to sleep lest she should lose control of her will which kept them out. But she seemed to have outgrown all that now.

'We were afraid at one time,' Mrs Hope confessed, 'that Mavis was going to believe she was a medium.' To what extent Mavis had outgrown this tendency remains to be recorded.

Late on a certain August evening Mavis Hope took out her canoe and paddled herself dreamily downstream under the stars. She had a whole reach of the river to herself, but never previously having had an accident she was supremely self-confident.

The mishap occurred with the suddenness peculiar to most mishaps. She lost her paddle, and stretched out despairingly to retrieve it.

Canoes are not built to allow people to stretch out far over either gunwale. All in a moment she found herself struggling in the water. Many people who spend half their lives on the water are unable to swim, and Mavis was able to swim only a stroke or two. Fortunately she was close in to the north bank. She struggled, choked, swallowed quarts of water, but managed, when almost at her last gasp, to grasp an overhanging tuft of grass. Somehow she dragged herself out and, lying prone on the bank, lost consciousness.

Two or three minutes later, a party of four young men, campers-out up the river, came by in a punt. Mavis's white dress revealed her in the darkness, and something in the attitude of the prone figure moved them to turn the nose of the punt towards the bank and make investigations. After a little while they managed to revive her. They were strangers to the neighbourhood and were thus quite unaware of the girl's identity.

'How did it happen'?' they asked her, as soon as she was fit to speak.

She stared at them dazedly, a far-off look in her eyes, and then answered very distinctly. But the voice was not the voice of Mavis Hope. Nor was the string of epithets which fell from her lips characteristic of a young woman of refinement.

'He pushed me in, the swine!' she concluded vehemently.

The four young men became instantly excited.

'Who pushed you in?'

'Reggie Lockland. He lives over there. That big house where you see the lights.'

'Good God! What's your name, if you don't mind telling us?'

And she answered very distinctly: 'Dolly Frewan.'

They had never heard of Dolly Frewan. Nor for that matter had Mavis in her normal state. They asked where she lived that they might take her home, and she gave them Dolly Frewan's old address.

The four young men helped her into the punt, and one of them poled it over to the opposite bank close to the Lockland's house. They were high-spirited young men, and determined, before taking the drenched girl home, to confront her with her would-be murderer. They marched up to the Lockland's front door, assisting her between them, and one of them pressed the bell.

As luck would have it a new maid answered the bell. She stood flabbergasted while the four young men harangued her. Mr Reggie, she tried to explain, hadn't been out all the evening. But they would not hear her. Bluntly they told her to go and fetch him. The maid went upstairs to the study which Reggie had recently acquired for his private use.

'There's a lady downstairs who's been in the river,' she jerked out, 'and four young gentlemen who want to see you. She says you pushed her in. She says her name's Dolly Frewan.'

Reggie Lockland's face went livid, his lips writhed and emitted one short whistling cry. He fell like a man shot dead, his forehead striking the edge of the table before him. It was thus not until the last moment of his life that he knew the truth.

Meanwhile Mavis, dazedly stroking her forehead, was giving another version of the affair to four very embarrassed young men.

'What have I been saying? It's all wrong. Nobody pushed me in. I overturned a canoe. My name is Hope . . . Mavis Hope . . .'

The Sweeper

It seemed to Tessa Winyard that Miss Ludgate's strangest characteristic was her kindness to beggars. This was something more than a little peculiar in a nature which, to be sure, presented a surface like a mountain range of unexpected peaks and valleys; for there was a thin streak of meanness in her. One caught glimpses of it here and there to be traced a little way and lost, like a thin elusive vein in a block of marble. One week she would pay the household bills without a murmur; the next she would simmer over them in a mild rage, questioning the smallest item, and suggesting the most absurd little economies which she would have been the first to condemn later if Mrs Finch the housekeeper had ever taken her at her word. She was rich enough to be indifferent, but old enough to be crotchety.

Miss Ludgate gave very sparsely to local charities, and those good busybodies who went forth at different times with subscription lists and tales of good causes often visited her and came empty away. She had plausible, transparent excuses for keeping her purse-strings tight. Hospitals should be state-aided; schemes for assisting the local poor destroyed thrift; we had heathen of our own to convert, and needed to send no missionaries abroad.

Yet she was sometimes overwhelmingly generous in her spasmodic charities to individuals, and her kindness to itinerant beggars was proverbial among their fraternity. Her neighbours were not grateful to her for this, for it was said that she encouraged every doubtful character who came that way.

When she first agreed to come on a month's trial Tessa Winyard had known that she would find Miss Ludgate difficult, doubting whether she would be able to retain the post of companion, and, still more, if she would want to retain it. The thing was not arranged through the reading and answering of an advertisement. Tessa knew a married niece of the old lady who, while recommending the young girl to her ancient kinswoman, was able to give Tessa hints as to the nature and treatment of the old lady's crochets. So she came to the house well instructed and not quite as a stranger.

Tessa came under the spell of the house from the moment when she entered it for the first time. She had an ingrained romantic love of old country mansions, and Billingdon Abbots, although nothing was left of the original priory after which it was named, was old enough to be worshipped. It was mainly Jacobean, but some eighteenth-century owner, a devotee of the then fashionable cult of Italian architecture, had covered the facade with stucco and added a pillared portico. It was probably the same owner who had erected a summer house to the design of a Greek temple at the end of a walk between nut bushes, and who was responsible for the imitation ruin—to which Time had since added the authentic touch—beside the reedy fishpond at the rear of the house. Likely enough, thought Tessa, who knew the period, that same romantic squire was wont to engage an imitation 'hermit' to meditate beside the spurious ruin on moonlight nights.

The gardens around the house were well wooded, and thus lent the house itself an air of melancholy and the inevitable slight atmosphere of damp and darkness. And here and there, in the most unexpected places, were garden gods, mostly broken and all in need of scouring. Tessa soon discovered these stone ghosts quite unexpectedly, and nearly always with a leap and tingle of surprise. A noseless Hermes confronted one at the turn of a shady walk; Demeter, minus a hand, stood half hidden by laurels, still keeping vigil for Persephone; a dancing faun stood poised and caught in a frozen caper by the gate of the walled-in kitchen garden; beside a small stone pond a satyr leered from his pedestal, as if waiting for a naiad to break the surface.

The interior of the house was at first a little awe-inspiring to Tessa. She loved pretty things, but she was inclined to be afraid of furniture and pictures which seemed to her to be coldly beautiful and conscious of their own intrinsic values. Everything was highly polished, spotless and speckless, and the reception rooms had an air of state apartments thrown open for the inspection of the public.

The hall was square and galleried, and one could look straight up to the top storey and see the slanting balustrades of three staircases. Two suits of armour faced one across a parquet floor, and on the walls were three or four portraits by Lely and Kneller, those once fashionable painters of court beauties whose works have lost favour with the collectors of to-day. The dining-room was long, rectangular and severe, furnished only with a Cromwellian table and chairs and a great plain sideboard gleaming with silver candelabra. Two large seventeenth-century portraits by unknown members of the Dutch School were the only decorations bestowed on the panelled walls, and the window curtains were brown to match the one strip of carpet which the long table almost exactly covered.

Less monastic, but almost as severe and dignified, was the drawing-room in which Tessa spent most of her time with Miss Ludgate. The boudoir was a homelier room, containing such human things as photographs of living people, work-baskets, friendly armchairs and a cosy, feminine atmosphere; but Miss Ludgate preferred more often to sit in state in her great drawing-room with the 'Portrait of Miss Olivia Ludgate', by Gainsborough, the Chippendale furniture, and the cabinet of priceless china. It was as if she realized that she was but the guardian of her treasures, and wanted to have them within sight now that her term of guardianship was drawing to a close.

She must have been well over eighty, Tessa thought; for she was very small and withered and frail, with that almost porcelain delicacy peculiar to certain very old ladies. Winter and summer she wore a white woollen shawl inside the house, thick or thin according to the season, which matched in colour and to some extent in texture her soft and still plentiful hair. Her face and hands were yellow-brown with the veneer of old age, but her hands were blue-veined, light and delicate, so that her fingers seemed over-weighted by the simplest rings. Her eyes were blue and still piercing, and her mouth, once beautiful, was caught up at the corners by puckerings of the upper lip, and looked grim in repose. Her voice had not shrilled and always she spoke very slowly with an unaffected precision, as one who knew that she had only to be understood to be obeyed and therefore took care always to be understood.

Tessa spent her first week with Miss Ludgate without knowing whether or not she liked the old lady, or whether or not she was afraid of her. Nor was she any wiser with regard to Miss Ludgate's sentiments towards herself.

Their relations were much as they might have been had Tessa been a child and Miss Ludgate a new governess suspected of severity. Tessa was on her best behaviour, doing as she was told and thinking before she spoke, as children should and generally do not. At times it occurred to her to wonder that Miss Ludgate had not sought to engage an older woman, for in the cold formality of that first week's intercourse she wondered what gap in the household she was supposed to fill, and what return she was making for her wage and board.

Truth to tell, Miss Ludgate wanted to see somebody young about the house, even if she could share with her companion no more than the common factors of their sex and their humanity. The servants were all old retainers kept faithful to her by rumours of legacies. Her relatives were few and immersed in their own affairs. The house and the bulk of the property from which she derived her income were held in trust for an heir appointed by the same will which had given her a life interest in the estate. It saved her from the transparent attentions of any fortune-hunting nephew or niece, but it kept her lonely and starved for young companionship.

It happened that Tessa was able to play the piano quite reasonably well and that she had an educated taste in music. So had Miss Ludgate, who had been a performer of much the same quality until the time came when her rebel fingers stiffened with rheumatism. So the heavy grand piano, which had been scrupulously kept in tune, was silent no longer, and Miss Ludgate regained an old lost pleasure. It should be added that Tessa was twenty-two and, with no pretensions to technical beauty, was rich in commonplace good looks which were enhanced by perfect health and the freshness of her youth. She looked her best in candlelight, with her slim hands—they at least would have pleased an artist—hovering like white moths over the keyboard of the piano.

When she had been with Miss Ludgate a week, the old lady addressed her for the first time as 'Tessa'. She added: 'I hope you intend to stay with me, my dear. It will be dull for you, and I fear you will often find me a bother. But I shan't take up all your time, and I daresay you will be able to find friends and amusements.'

So Tessa stayed on, and beyond the probationary month. She was a soft-hearted girl who gave her friendship easily but always sincerely. She tried to like everybody who liked her, and generally succeeded. It would be hard to analyse the quality of the friendship between the two women, but certainly it existed and at times they were able to touch hands over the barrier between youth and age. Miss Ludgate inspired in Tessa a queer tenderness.

With all her wealth and despite her domineering manner, she was a pathetic and lonely figure. She reminded Tessa of some poor actress playing the part of Queen, wearing the tawdry crown jewels, uttering commands which the other mummers obeyed like automata; while all the while there awaited her the realities of life at the fall of the curtain—the wet streets, the poor meal and the cold and comfortless lodging.

It filled Tessa with pity to think that here, close beside her, was a living, breathing creature, still clinging to life, who must, in the course of nature, so soon let go her hold. Tessa could think: 'Fifty years hence I shall be seventy-two, and there's no reason why I shouldn't live till then.' She wondered painfully how it must feel to be unable to look a month hence with average confidence, and to regard every nightfall as the threshold of a precarious tomorrow.

Tessa would have found life very dull but for the complete change in her surroundings. She had been brought up in a country vicarage, one of seven brothers and sisters who had worn each other's clothes, tramped the carpets threadbare, mishandled the cheap furniture, broken everything frangible except their parents' hearts, and had somehow tumbled into adolescence. The unwonted 'grandeur' of living with Miss Ludgate flavoured the monotony.

We have her writing home to her 'Darling Mother' as follows: I expect when I get back home again our dear old rooms will look absurdly small. I thought at first that the house was huge, and every room as big as a barrack-room—not that I've ever been in a barrack-room! But I'm getting used to it now, and really it isn't so enormous as I thought. Huge compared with ours, of course, but not so big as Lord Branboume's house, or even Colonel Exted's.

Really, though, it's a darling old place and might have come out of one of those books in which there's a Mystery, and a Sliding Panel, and the heroine's a nursery governess who marries the Young Baronet. But there's no mystery that I've heard of, although I like to pretend there is, and even if I were the nursery governess there's no young baronet within a radius of miles. But at least it ought to have a traditional ghost, although, since I haven't heard of one, it's probably deficient even in that respect! I don't like to ask Miss Ludgate because, although she's a dear, there are questions I couldn't ask her. She might believe in ghosts and it might scare her to talk about them; or she mightn't, and then she'd be furious with me for talking rubbish. Of course, I know it's all rubbish but it would be very nice to know that we were supposed to be haunted by a nice Grey Lady—of, say—about the period of Queen Anne. But if we're haunted by nothing else, we're certainly haunted by tramps.

Her letter went on to describe the numerous daily visits of those nomads of the English countryside, who beg and steal on their way from workhouse to workhouse; those queer, illogical, feckless beings who prefer the most intense miseries and hardships to the comparative comforts attendant on honest work. Three or four was a day's average of such callers, and not one went empty away. Mrs Finch had very definite orders and she carried them out with the impassive face of a perfect subject of discipline. When there was no spare food there was the pleasanter alternative of money which could be transformed into liquor at the nearest inn.

Tessa was forever meeting these vagrants in the drive. Male and female they differed in a hundred ways; some still trying to cling to the last rags of self-respect, others obscene, leering, furtive, potential criminals who lacked the courage to rise above petty theft. Most faces were either evil or carried the rolling eyes and lewd loose mouth of the semi-idiot, but they were all alike in their personal uncleanliness and in the insolence of their bearing.

Tessa grew used to receiving from them direct and insolent challenges of the eyes, familiar nods, blatant grins. In their several ways they told her that she was nobody and that if she hated to see them, so much the better. They knew she was an underling, subject to dismissal, whereas they, for some occult reason, were always the welcome guests. Tessa resented their presence and their dumb insolence and secretly raged against Miss Ludgate for encouraging them. They were the sewer-rats of society, foul, predatory and carrying disease from village to village and from town to town.

The girl knew something of the struggles of the decent poor. Her upbringing in a country vicarage had given her intimate knowledge of farm hands and builders' labourers, the tragic poverty of their homes, their independence and their gallant struggles for existence. On Miss Ludgate's estate there was more than one family living on bread and potatoes and getting not too much of either. Yet the old lady had no sympathy for them, and gave unlimited largess to the undeserving. In the ditches outside the park it was always possible to find a loaf or two of bread flung there by some vagrant who had feasted more delicately on the proceeds of a visit to the tradesmen's door.

It was not for Tessa to speak to Miss Ludgate on the subject. Indeed, she knew that—in the phraseology of the servants' hall—it was as much as her place was worth. But she did mention it to Mrs Finch, whose duty was to provide food and drink, or, failing those, money.

Mrs Finch, taciturn through her environment but still with an undercurrent of warmth, replied at first with the one pregnant word. 'Orders!' After a moment she added: 'The mistress has her own good reasons for doing it—or thinks she has.'

It was late summer when Tessa first took up her abode at Billingdon Abbots, and sweet lavender, that first herald of the approach of autumn, was already blooming in the gardens. September came and the first warning gleams of yellow showed among the trees. Spiked chestnut husks opened and dropped their polished brown fruit. At evenings the ponds and the trout stream exhaled pale, low-hanging mists. There was a cold snap in the air.

By looking from her window every morning Tessa marked on the trees the inexorable progress of the year. Day by day the green tints lessened as the yellow increased. Then yellow began to give place to gold and brown and red. Only the hollies and the laurels stood fast against the advancing tide. There came an evening when Miss Ludgate appeared for the first time in her winter shawl. She seemed depressed and said little during dinner, and afterwards in the drawing-room, when she had taken out and arranged a pack of patience cards preparatory to beginning her evening game, she suddenly leaned her elbows on the table and rested her face between her hands.

'Aren't you well, Miss Ludgate?' Tessa asked anxiously.

She removed her hands and showed her withered old face. Her eyes were piteous, fear-haunted and full of shadows.

'I am very much as usual, my dear,' she said. 'You must bear with me. My bad time of the year is just approaching. If I can live until the end of November I shall last another year. But I don't know yet—I don't know.'

'Of course you're not going to die this year,' said Tessa, with a robust note of optimism which she had found useful in soothing frightened children.

'If I don't die this autumn it will be the next or some other autumn,' quavered the old voice, it will be in the autumn that I shall die. I know that. I know that.'

'But how can you know?' Tessa asked, with just the right note of gentle incredulity.

'I know it. What does it matter how I know? . . . Have many leaves fallen yet?'

'Hardly any as yet,' said Tessa. 'There has been very little wind.'

'They will fall presently,' said Miss Ludgate. 'Very soon now. . .

Her voice trailed away, but presently she rallied, picked up the miniature playing cards and began her game.

Two days later it rained heavily all the morning and throughout the earlier part of the afternoon. Just as the light was beginning to wane, half a gale of wind sprang up, and showers of yellow leaves, circling and eddying at the wind's will, began to find their way to earth through the level slant of the rain. Miss Ludgate sat watching them, her eyes dull with the suffering of despair, until the lights were turned on and the blinds were drawn.

During dinner the wind dropped again and the rain ceased. Tessa afterwards peeped between the blinds to see still silhouettes of trees against the sky, and a few stars sparkling palely. It promised after all to be a fine night. As before, Miss Ludgate got out her patience cards, and Tessa picked up a book and waited to be bidden go to the piano. There was silence in the room save for intermittent sounds of cards being laid with a snap upon the polished surface of the table, and occasional dry rustlings as Tessa turned the pages of her book.

. . . When she first heard it Tessa could not truthfully have said. It seemed to her that she had gradually become conscious of the sounds in the garden outside, and when at last they had so forced themselves upon her attention as to set her wondering what caused them it was impossible for her to guess how long they had actually been going on.

Tessa closed the book over her fingers and listened. The sounds were crisp, dry, long drawn out and rhythmic. There was an equal pause after each one. It was rather like listening to the leisurely brushing of a woman's long hair. What was it? An uneven surface being scratched by something crisp and pliant? Then Tessa knew. On the long path behind the house which travelled the whole length of the building somebody was sweeping up the fallen leaves with a stable broom. But what a time to sweep up leaves!

She continued to listen. Now that she had identified the sounds they were quite unmistakable. She would not have had to guess twice had it not been dark outside, and the thought of a gardener showing such devotion to duty as to work at that hour had at first been rejected by her subconscious mind. She looked up, with the intention of making some remark to Miss Ludgate—and she said nothing.

Miss Ludgate sat listening intently, her face half-turned towards the windows and slightly raised, her eyes upturned. Her whole attitude was one of strained rigidity, expressive of a tension rather dreadful to see in one so old. Tessa not only listened, she now watched.

There was a movement in the unnaturally silent room. Miss Ludgate had turned her head, and now showed her companion a white face of woe and doom-ridden eyes. Then, in a flash, her expression changed. Tessa knew that Miss Ludgate had caught her listening to the sounds from the path outside, and that for some reason the old lady was annoyed with her for having heard them. But why? And why that look of terror on the poor white old face?

'Won't you play something, Tessa?'

Despite the note of interrogation, the words were an abrupt command, and Tessa knew it. She was to drown the noise of sweeping from outside, because, for some queer reason, Miss Ludgate did not want her to hear it. So, tactfully, she played pieces which allowed her to make liberal use of the loud pedal.

After half an hour Miss Ludgate rose, gathered her shawl tighter about her shoulders, and hobbled to the door, pausing on the way to say good night to Tessa.

Tessa lingered in the room alone and re-seated herself before the piano. A minute or two elapsed before she began to strum softly and absent-mindedly. Why did Miss Ludgate object to her hearing that sound of sweeping from the path outside? It had ceased now, or she would have peeped out to see who actually was at work. Had Miss Ludgate some queer distaste for seeing fallen leaves lying about, and was she ashamed because she was keeping a gardener at work at that hour? But it was unlike Miss Ludgate to mind what people thought of her; besides, she rose late in the morning, and there would be plenty of time to brush away the leaves before the mistress of the house could set eyes on them. And then, why was Miss Ludgate so terrified? Had it anything to do with her queer belief that she would die in the autumn?

On her way to bed Tessa smiled gently to herself for having tried to penetrate to the secret places of a warped mind which was over eighty years old. She had just seen another queer phase of Miss Ludgate, and all of such seemed inexplicable.

The night was still calm and promised so to remain.

'There won't be many more leaves down to-night,' Tessa reflected as she undressed.

But when next morning she sauntered out into the garden before breakfast the long path which skirted the rear of the house was still thickly littered with them, and Toy, the second gardener, was busy among them with a barrow and one of those birch stable brooms which, in mediaeval imaginations, provided steeds for witches.

'Hullo!' exclaimed Tessa. 'What a lot of leaves must have come down last night!'

Toy ceased sweeping and shook his head.

'No, Miss. This 'ere little lot come down with the wind early part o' the evenin'.'

'But surely they were all swept up. I heard somebody at work here after nine o'clock. Wasn't it you?'

The man grinned.

'You catch any of us at work after nine o'clock, Miss!' he said. 'No, Miss, nobody's touched 'em till now. 'Tes thankless work, too. So soon as you've swept up one lot there's another waitin'. Not a hundred men could keep this 'ere garden tidy this time o' the year.'

Tessa said nothing more and went thoughtfully into the house. The sweeping was continued off and on all day, for more leaves descended, and a bonfire built up on the waste ground beyond the kitchen garden wafted its fragrance over to the house.

That evening Miss Ludgate had a fire made up in the boudoir and announced to Tessa that they would sit there before and after dinner. But it happened that the chimney smoked, and after coughing and grumbling, and rating Mrs Finch on the dilatoriness and inefficiency of sweeps, the old lady went early to bed.

It was still too early for Tessa to retire. Having been left to herself she remembered a book which she had left in the drawing-room, and with which she purposed sitting over the dining-room fire. Hardly had she taken two steps past the threshold of the drawing-room when she came abruptly to a halt and stood listening. She could not doubt the evidence of her ears. In spite of what Toy had told her, and that it was now after half-past nine, somebody was sweeping the path outside.

She tiptoed to the window and peeped out between the blinds. Bright moonlight silvered the garden, but she could see nothing. Now, however, that she was near the window she could locate the sounds more accurately, and they seemed to proceed from a spot further down the path which was hidden from her by the angle of the window setting. There was a door just outside the room giving access to the garden, but for no reason that she could name she felt strangely unwilling to go out and look at the mysterious Worker.

With the strangest little cold thrill she was aware of a distinct preference for seeing him— for the first time, at least—from a distance.

Then Tessa remembered a landing window, and, after a little hesitation she went silently and on tiptoe upstairs to the first floor, and down a passage on the left of the stairhead. Here moonlight penetrated a window and threw a pale blue screen upon the opposite wall. Tessa fumbled with the window fastenings, raised the sash softly and silently and leaned out.

On the path below her, but some yards to her left and close to the angle of the house, a man was slowly and rhythmically sweeping with a stable broom. The broom swung and struck the path time after time with a soft, crisp swish, and the strokes were as regular as those of the pendulum of some slow old clock.

From her angle of observation she was unable to see most of the characteristics of the figure underneath. It was that of a working man, for there was something in the silhouette subtly suggestive of old and baggy clothes. But apart from all else there was something queer, something odd and unnatural, in the scene on which she gazed. She knew that there was something lacking, something that she should have found missing at the first glance, yet for her life she could not have said what it was.

From below some gross omission blazed up at her, and though she was acutely aware that the scene lacked something which she had every right to expect to see, her senses groped for it in vain; although the lack of something which should have been there and was not, was as obvious as a burning pyre at midnight. She knew that she was watching the gross defiance of some natural law, but what law she did not know. Suddenly sick and dizzy, she withdrew her head.

All the cowardice in Tessa's nature urged her to go to bed, to forget what she had seen and to refrain from trying to remember what she had not seen. But the other Tessa, the Tessa who despised cowards, and was herself capable under pressure of rising to great heights of courage, stayed and urged. Under her breath she talked to herself, as she always did when any crisis found her in a state of indecision.

'Tessa, you coward! How dare you be afraid! Go down at once and see who it is and what's queer about him. He can't eat you!'

So the two Tessas imprisoned in the one body stole downstairs again, and the braver Tessa was angry with their common heart for thumping so hard and trying to weaken her. But she unfastened the door and stepped out into the moonlight.

The Sweeper was still at work close to the angle of the house, nearby where the path ended and a green door gave entrance to the stable yard. The path was thick with leaves, and the girl, advancing uncertainly with her hands to her breasts, saw that he was making little progress with his work. The broom rose and fell and audibly swept the path, but the dead leaves lay fast and still beneath it. Yet it was not this that she had noticed from above. There was still that unseizable Something missing.

Her footfalls made little noise on the leaf-strewn path, but they became audible to the Sweeper while she was still half a dozen yards from him. He paused in his work and turned and looked at her.

He was a tall, lean man with a white cadaverous face and eyes that bulged like huge rising bubbles as they regarded her. It was a foul, suffering face which he showed to Tessa, a face whose misery could—and did—inspire loathing and a hitherto unimagined horror, but never pity. He was clad in the meanest rags, which seemed to have been cast at random over his emaciated body. The hands grasping the broom seemed no more than bones and skin.

He was so thin, thought Tessa, that he was almost—and here she paused in thought, because she found herself hating the word which tried to force itself into her mind. But it had its way, and blew in on a cold wind of terror. Yes, he was almost transparent, she thought, and sickened at the word which had come to have a new and vile meaning for her.

They faced each other through a fraction of eternity not to be measured by seconds; and then Tessa heard herself scream. It flashed upon her now, the strange, abominable detail of the figure which confronted her—the Something Missing which she had noticed, without actually seeing, from above. The path was flooded with moonlight, but the Visitant had no shadow. And fast upon this vile discovery she saw dimly through it the ivy stirring upon the wall. Then as unbidden thoughts rushed to tell her that the Thing was not of this world, and that it was not holy, and the sudden knowledge wrung that scream from her, so she was left suddenly and dreadfully alone. The spot where the Thing had stood was empty save for the moonlight and the shallow litter of leaves.

Tessa had no memory of returning to the house. Her next recollection was of finding herself in the hall, faint and gasping and sobbing. Even as she approached the stairs she saw a light dancing on the wall above and wondered what fresh horror was to confront her. But it was only Mrs Finch coming downstairs in a dressing-gown, candle in hand, an incongruous but a very comforting sight.

'Oh, it's you, Miss Tessa,' said Mrs Finch reassured. She held the candle lower and peered down at the sobbing girl. 'Why, whatever is the matter? Oh, Miss Tessa, Miss Tessa! You haven't never been outside, have you?'

Tessa sobbed and choked and tried to speak.

'I've seen—I've seen'

Mrs Finch swiftly descended the remaining stairs, and put an arm around the shuddering girl.

'Hush, my dear, my dear! I know what you've seen. You didn't ought never to have gone out. I've seen it too, once—but only once, thank God.'

'What is it?' Tessa faltered.

'Never you mind, my dear. Now don't be frightened. It's all over now. He doesn't come here for you. It's the mistress he wants. You've nothing to fear, Miss Tessa. Where was he when you saw him?'

'Close to the end of the path, near the stable gate.'

Mrs Finch threw up her hands.

'Oh, the poor mistress—the poor mistress! Her time's shortening! The end's nigh, now!'

'I can't bear any more,' Tessa sobbed; and then she contradicted herself, clinging to Mrs Finch, 'I must know. I can't rest until I know. Tell me everything.'

'Come into my parlour, my dear, and I'll make a cup of tea. We can both do with it, I think. But you'd best not know. At least not to-night, Miss Tessa—not to-night.'

'I must,' whispered Tessa, 'if I'm ever to have any peace.'

The fire was still burning behind a guard in the housekeeper's parlour, for Mrs Finch had only gone up to bed a few minutes since. There was water still warm in the brass kettle, and in a few minutes the tea was ready. Tessa sipped and felt the first vibrations of her returning courage, and presently looked inquiringly at Mrs Finch.

'I'll tell you, Miss Tessa,' said the old housekeeper, 'if it'll make you any easier. But don't let the mistress know as I've ever told you.'

Tessa inclined her head and gave the required promise.

'You don't know why,' Mrs Finch began in a low voice, 'the mistress gives to every beggar, deserving or otherwise. The reason comes into what I'm going to tell you. Miss Ludgate wasn't always like that—not until up to about fifteen years ago.

'She was old then, but active for her age, and very fond of gardenin'.

Late one afternoon in the autumn while she was cutting some late roses, a beggar came to the tradesmen's door. Sick and ill and starved, he looked—but there, you've seen him. He was a bad lot, we found out afterwards, but I was sorry for him, and I was just going to risk givin' him some food without orders, when up comes Miss Ludgate. "What's this?" she says.

'He whined something about not being able to get work. ' "Work!" says the mistress. "You don't want work—you want charity. If you want to eat," she says, "you shall, but you shall work first. There's a broom," she says, "and there's a path littered with leaves. Start sweeping up at the top, and when you come to the end you can come and see me."

'Well, he took the broom, and a few minutes later I heard a shout from Miss Ludgate and come hurryin' out. There was the man lyin' at the top of the path where he'd commenced sweeping, and he'd collapsed and fallen down. I didn't know then as he was dying, but he did, and he gave Miss Ludgate a look as I shall never forget.

' "When I've swept to the end of the path," he says, "I'll come for you, my lady, and we'll feast together. Only see as you're ready to be fetched when I come." Those were his last words. He was buried by the parish, and it gave Miss Ludgate such a turn that she ordered something to be given to every beggar who came, and not one of 'em to be asked to do a stroke of work.

'But next autumn, when the leaves began to fall, he came back and started sweeping, right at the top of the path, round about where he died. We've all heard him and most of us have seen him. Year after year he's come back and swept with his broom which just makes a brushing noise and hardly stirs a leaf. But each year he's been getting nearer and nearer to the end of the path, and when he gets right to the end—well, I wouldn't like to be the mistress, with all her money.'

It was three evenings later, just before the hour fixed for dinner, that the Sweeper completed his task. That is to say, if one reposes literal belief in Mrs Finch's story.

The servants heard somebody burst open the tradesmen's door, and, having rushed out into the passage, two of them saw that the door was open but found no one there. Miss Ludgate was already in the drawing-room, but Tessa was still upstairs, dressing for dinner. Presently Mrs Finch had occasion to enter the drawing-room to speak to her mistress; and her screams warned the household of what had happened. Tessa heard them just as she was ready to go downstairs, and she rushed into the drawing-room a few moments later.

Miss Ludgate was sitting upright in her favourite chair. Her eyes were open, but she was quite dead; and in her eyes there was something that Tessa could not bear to see.

Withdrawing her own gaze from that fixed stare of terror and recognition she saw something on the carpet and presently stooped to pick it up. It was a little yellow leaf, damp and pinched and frayed, and but for her own experience and Mrs Finch's tale she might have wondered how it had come to be there. She dropped it, shuddering, for it looked as if it had been picked up by, and had afterwards fallen from, the birch twigs of a stable broom.

A.M. Burrage – The Life And Times.

Alfred McLelland Burrage, better known as simply AM Burrage, was born in Hillingdon, Middlesex on July 1st, 1889, to Alfred Sherrington Burrage and Mary E. Burrage. On his Father's side writing already ran in the family's blood as both he and an uncle, Edwin Harcourt Burrage, were writers of the then very popular boys' magazine fiction.

Life in late Victorian times was by no means easy and writing has always been a precarious career for most. For an insight into the young AM and his surroundings it is interesting to see how certain facts were captured in the 1891 census when he was aged one. The family is listed as living at Uxbridge Common in Hillingdon. His father is 40 and his mother 36. In the next census of 1901, and with it the end of the Victorian era, the family has moved to 1

Park Villa, Newbury. In that time his father has aged 17 years his mother 6 years and young AM has disappeared from the records. It's almost a precursor to one of his stories.

There is little documented about his growing up and education. What we can glean though is something about his environment. His neighbours were varied: a tailor's journeyman, a corn porter, a lodging-house keeper and a grocer's assistant. Nothing particularly illustrious, so times cannot have been as rosy as they should, especially in the light of his Father's hard work. Alfred Sherrington wrote for The Boy's World, Our Boys' Paper, The Boys of England, and various others. He also appears to have written under the pseudonym Philander Jackson and edited The Boys' Standard and that one of his more celebrated pieces was a retelling of the story of Sweeney Todd entitled "The String of Peals; or, Passages from the Life of Sweeney Todd, the Demon Barber".

Sadly Alfred Sherrington Burrage died in 1906. There is a biographical note in Lloyd's Magazine, from 1921, which suggests that young Alfred McLelland was studying at St. Augustine's, the Catholic Foundation School in Ramsgate, and most probably away from home at the time.

A.M. Burrage was 16 years old when he had his first story published; the same year as his father's death, in the prestigious boys' paper, Chums. It was a great start to his professional career and whether doors had been opened by his father and family or not the young man's career now had to stand on its own. He was now primary provider for the household and this was the only way he could do it. His Mother, sister and aunt must be provided for.

Magazine fiction was his family's blood and business and for A. M. Burrage, business was good. He established himself as a competent and creative writer and was busy writing stories and articles on a weekly basis for publications such as Boys' Friend Weekly, Boys' Herald, Comic Life, Vanguard, Dreadnought, Triumph Library Cheer Boys Cheer, and Gem, under the pseudonym 'Cooee'.

However, unlike his father and uncle who had remained firmly and easily categorised as boys' writers, he had his sights set on the more well regarded, more lucrative, adult market. Burrage was aided in his early years as a professional writer by Isobel Thorne of the off-Fleet Street publishing firm Shurey's. Her publications have been characterised as "low in price, modest in payments, but whose readers were avid for romance, thrills, sensation, strong characterisation and neat plotting", and this estimation of her publications also fits nicely the description of Burrage's own writing at that time. For a young writer this sort of readership was vital, and the modest wages he received were bolstered by the exposure the publications brought him. Burrage was certainly helped by Thorne's use of young writers.

At the time Burrage was beginning to really establish himself as a writer, the entire magazine fiction scene was benefiting from what we would now see as disruptive influences: new printing techniques, a growing readership with more disposable income and leisure time and other media failing to provide – though obviously movies and such were only in their infancy at the time. The market was lively and commercial, and the readership interested, excitable and willing to pay. P. G. Wodehouse, of Jeeves fame, recalls these years:

We might get turned down by the Strand, but there was always the hope of landing with Nash's, the Story-teller, the London, the Royal, the Red, the Yellow, Cassell's, the New, the Novel, the Grand, the Pall Mall, and the Windsor, not to mention Blackwood's, Cornhill, Chambers's and probably about a dozen more I've forgotten.

With War clouds darkening the skies of Europe in 1914 Burrage was firmly established as a magazine writer, securing publication in London Magazine and The Storyteller, which were both highly prestigious publications. Alongside he had plenty printed in less illustrious publications such as Short Stories Illustrated.

By now Burrage, a young man of twenty-four-year-was eligible for the Armed Services. Under the 'Derby Scheme' he confirmed that he was available for service if called upon in December 1915. Conscription was to follow shortly though, by that time, Burrage had already voluntarily enrolled in the Artists Rifles.

The significance of Burrage's decision to join the Artists Rifles is made clear by the nature of the unit itself. They formed in the middle of the nineteenth century, a group of volunteer artists comprising musicians, writers, painters and engravers. Minerva and Mars were their patrons, one of wisdom, arts, and defence, the other of war. The unit boasted several significant figures as ex-servicemen, including Dante Gabriel Rossetti, Algernon Charles Swinburne and William Morris. It was a popular unit with students and recent postgraduates, and the training was considered and extensive.

In Burrage's vivid, celebrated account of World War I entitled War is War, he insists that he was a volunteer and not a conscript, though as has already been noted, it is quite possible that his decision to join such a respected territorial unit may have been more of an effort to secure himself a more congenial army posting; had he waited for conscription, he would have had little choice over those with whom he was posted. Unlike poets Wilfred Owen or Edward Thomas, Burrage did not achieve a commission, and he suggests in War is War that this may be a result of his extremely unmilitary personality and his shortcomings as a soldier.

Add to this the fact that as the breadwinner for the family he was putting himself in harm's way. If anything were to happen to him the result on the family would be devastating. With the death of
Edwin Harcourt Burrage in 1916 it came even more starkly into focus.

Even though he was now a soldier he was still a writer and writers had to write. It also helped that it was a distraction from the mindless carnage around him. He experimented with various genres, excelling in the one that was to prove most lucrative for him; the light romance, in which a male character invariably meets a female character, there is a problem or hurdle to their being together, they overcome it and they live happily ever after. Burrage's talent for this formula was such that he could work seemingly endless minor variations from the same basic storyline and so he was able to keep writing a steady body of easy work.

He gives a fascinating account of the practicalities of writing such fiction during wartime in War is War, in which he remarks on the difficulties of censorship: "the problem of censorship was an acute one to me. It was well enough to write a story, but the difficulty was to get it censored. Officers were shy of tackling five thousand words or so, written in indelible pencil..." After some time he managed to find a chaplain who was willing to undertake the censorship. However, in order to secure this chaplain's favour and thus his services he was obliged to appear to be holy. Though he did so in earnest while he was with the chaplain, his efforts were dashed when the chaplain found him, sprawled on top of a young girl, and realised Burrage's piety to be a fraudulent con. As Burrage had anticipated, the reality of his behaviour ensured that this particular opportunity was swiftly ended. Resourceful to the last, though, he writes of his solution: "there were 'green envelopes' which could be sent away sealed and were liable only to censorship at the base, but these were only sparingly issued... I met an A.S.C. lorry driver who had stolen enough green envelopes to last me for the rest of the war; and since he only wanted two francs for them I was free of the censorship from that day forward."

Although we know that Burrage had his family to support at home as an incentive to keep writing, at times in War is War he reveals a more intimate aspect of his relationship with his work.

"It was a great relief to me to write when it was at all possible – to sit down and lose myself in that pleasant old world I used to know and pretend to myself that there never had been a war. Some of my editors seemed of the opinion that we were not suffering from one now. One used to write to me saying "Couldn't you let me have one of your light, charming love stories of country house life by next Thursday." I would get these letters in the trenches during the usual 'morning hate' when my fingers were too numb to hold a pencil, when I was worn out with work and sleeplessness, and when I was extremely doubtful if there ever would be another Thursday".

Writing is a useful therapy and for Burrage it provided a means to escape if only for a short time to a world that he could control and move at will. With the misery and harsh conditions of the War dragging on he was eventually invalided and so he returned to England.

One of the best insights we have as to the character which Burrage presented on his return from the war is to be found in Lloyd's's 1920 publication of Captain Dorry, one of Burrage's story series. In that publication there was included a brief sketch of Burrage, describing his personality.

A.M. BURRAGE is the type of young man who might very well walk out of one of his own stories. He commenced yarn-spinning as a boy of fifteen at St Augustine's, Ramsgate, writing stories of school life to provide himself with pocket-money. Since then he has won his spurs as one of the most popular of magazine writers. Everything he does has charm and reflects his own romantic spirit – for he is incurably romantic and hopelessly lazy. It is his misfortune, although he would not admit it, that his work finds a too ready market. Nevertheless, his friends hope that one day he will wake up and do justice to himself.

Otherwise he may end up as a "best-seller", a fate which doubtless he contemplates with equanimity.

Despite the sketch's fairly accurate but negative summation of Burrage's literary output up to that point, some of his stories seem to exhibit a desire to write about more than just his usual romantic plots. The most immediate change of this nature is in his decision to bring some of his wartime experience into his work, despite being perfectly aware that such writing was not at all what his editors desired, for they feared it would upset and intimidate their readership.

An example of this can be found in "A Town of Memories", published in 1919 in Grand Magazine, in which he uses his well rehearsed romantic story with a slight shift of emphasis to explore his own return from the war and the general reception which soldiers received on their return. Following a young officer as he returns to the town in which he grew up, Burrage portrays an almost hostile environment into which he returns; he is unrecognised, and nobody pays any interest, respect or attention to him or his stories of the war, nor even to his reception of the Distinguished Service Order. Instead, the people of the town have their own interests and priorities with which to concern themselves. Though this contentious portrayal of post-war society certainly marks a slight shift in Burrage's writing, he returns to the romantic convention expected of him by reuniting the officer with a beautiful girl who had admired him throughout school. It would be harsh to not accept that market conditions expected one thing and to ignore them would mean turning his back on publications who still clamoured for his penmanship.

Another of Burrage's alternative directions is to be found in "The Recurring Tragedy", in which a General whose war tactics of attrition had been to the slaughtered cost of his soldiers, and he comes to re-imagine his own past as a Judas figure in a terrible vision. The Strange Career of Captain Dorry became a series for Lloyd's Magazine in 1920 about a gentleman crook and an ex-officer with a Military Cross who, idle in peacetime, meets a mysterious man called Fewgin whose business is in stolen goods and mind reading. Fewgin realises Dorry is a suitable candidate for recruitment into his gang of like-minded ex-military thieves, stealing only from "certain vampires who made money out of the war, and, by keeping up prices, are continuing to make money out of the peace". Again, in this motive, we see a glimpse of Burrage's own feelings on the war, as there is undoubtedly a bitterness towards those profiting from the suffering of others in such a manner. Fewgin justifies himself, saying:

"I help brave men who cannot help themselves. I give them a chance to get back a little of their own from the men who battened and fattened on them, who helped to starve their dependents while they were fighting, who smoked fat cigars in the haunts of their betters, and hoped the war might never end."

Burrage began to see slightly more success in the 1920s, achieving a couple of hard back publications entitled Some Ghost Stories and Poor Dear Esme. The latter, a comedy, concerns a boy who, for various reasons, is forced to disguise himself as a girl. Though these hard cover publications were a notable achievement, and one of which he was proud, the fact was that there was less money in it than in the magazines. In his history of the Strand

Magazine, Reginald Pound portrays Burrage around this time, likening him to his equally prolific contemporary Herbert Shaw, considering them "two Bohemian temperaments that suffused and at times confused gifts from which more was expected than come forth. They had a precise knowledge of the popular short story as the product of calculated design. Both privately despised it, though it was their living."

The early 1920s, and with them a boom in prosperity, hope and happiness, now brought with them an increase in demand for war stories. Rather than preferring to ignore the atrocities of the war, which had seemed the general attitude in the immediate post-war years, society became more interested and concerned with the manner in which the war was fought, and the greed and political battles which had necessitated such bloodshed. Burrage answered this demand in 1930 with his own epochal piece, War Is War. He published under the pseudonym 'Ex-Private X', saying "were it otherwise I could not tell the truth about myself", though its publisher, Victor Gollancz, "who published the book and greatly admired it, had to point out that the critics would hardly take the book seriously if it became known that the author earned his living producing two or three slushy love stories a week".

In one of a series of letters he wrote to his contemporary and fellow writer Dorothy Sayers, Burrage bemoans how War is War "promised to be a great success, but was only a moderate one". The book itself was received with reviews on both sides of the spectrum. Cyril Fall's War Books, a survey of post-war writing published in 1930, gives a clear indication as to why the critics were so mixed in reception of the book. He writes:

This book is extremely uneven in quality. The account of the attack at Paschendaele and of conditions at Cambrai after the great German counter-attack are very good indeed; in fact among the best of their kind. But the rest is disfigured by an unreasoned and unpleasant attack on superiors and all troops other than those of the front line, which is all the more astonishing because the author is inclined to harp upon his social position as compared with that of many of the officers with whom he came in contact. He does not use as much bad language as many writers on the War, but his methods of abuse will leave on some of his readers at least a worse impression than the most highly-spiced language.

Dorothy Sayers was the editor at Victor Gollanz for anthologies of ghost and horror stories which included stories by Burrage. She says, in one of her letters of Burrage's story The Waxwork, a piece beyond the nerves of the editors, "what you say about "The Waxwork" sounds very exciting, just the sort of thing I want. Our nerves are stronger than those of the editors of periodicals, and we will publish anything, so long as it does not bring us into conflict with the Home Secretary". Though their correspondence began as strictly business, Burrage's acquaintance with Atherton Fleming, Sayers's husband, allowed their interactions to become less formal and friendlier. Burrage wrote of Fleming "I hope to encounter him soon in one of the Fleet Street tea-shops". 'Tea-shop' being a popular euphemism for the pub, where both Burrage and Fleming could frequently be found, though their alcohol consumption came to damage both their health and their professions, with Burrage coming off the worse.

Happily for Burrage, as a result of being featured in one of Sayers's anthologies, The Waxwork became one of his best-known stories and it would grab the attention of the film companies several times down the years even becoming an episode in the TV series 'Alfred Hitchcock Presents'.

The developing friendship between Burrage and Sayers enabled him to reveal more details of his personal life, admitting to her his "neuritis at both ends (legs and eyes)", and hinting at his troubles with alcohol: "Fleet Street is not a good place for a man who delights in succumbing to temptation, and whose doctor says that even small doses of alcohol are poison to him". Sayers sympathises, replying that Fleming "agrees with you entirely about the temptations of Fleet Street; he has, however, succeeded, through sheer strength of character, in being able to drink soda-water in the face of all his fellow journalists".

In another of Burrage's letters, he apologises for a delay in sending proofs of a story, with the words:

I have had a pretty thin time lately through illness and anxiety. And for days on end haven't had the energy in me to write a letter, and when I had the energy to send a complete set of proofs to you I found I hadn't the postage money (This is when you take out your handkerchief and start sobbing). I owed my late agent over £1000, so I got practically nothing out of War is War. He stuck to it. Well, he is paid off now, and so are my arrears of income tax. All this took a toll of my very small earning capacity, and I have been sold up. This on top of something which promised to be a great success and was only a moderate one, was a bit too much for me. Still, in spite of sickness I am resilient and shall float again. "You can't keep a good man down," as the whale said about Jonah.

For a man who had so many stories in so many magazines, and was gaining pace in Sayers's anthologies as a talented writer of horror stories, his income will have been far higher than the then average wage, and yet as he says, he finds himself short of money.

Several questions are left unanswered about his personal life. It is unclear whether he was still supporting family, or whether he spent the majority of his money on alcohol, or whether he chose to conceal his true fortunes from those around him. Perhaps most incongruous is the apparent absence of a wife; though his death certificate indicates that he had one, listed as H.A. Burrage, he seems never to mention her to Sayers.

He was around forty-two when he wrote that apology letter to Sayers, though in tone and circumstance it seems to be from a man in a far later stage of his life.

Burrage continued writing until his death in 1956, and continued to be prolifically published. Indeed, the Evening News alone published some forty of his stories between 1950-56. His death is recorded at Edgware General Hospital on 18th December, and the causes of his death are recorded as congestive cardiac failure, arteriosclerosis and chronic bronchitis. He was sixty-seven years old, and his last address is listed as 105 Vaughan Road, Harrow.

Though his name is not often remembered in lists of prominent writers of his time, or even it's genres, his ghost stories are highly regarded by critics and fans alike, while his life story tells us much about the trials and stresses placed on authors during and after the war, and on soldiers returning from that war. His reluctant acceptance that the money was in the magazines while the esteem was in the poorly-paying hard covers, and his persistence as a writer, speak of a determined man, doomed to circumstance yet living as best he could.

In ending A.M Burrage wrote a few sentences which best sum up two things. Firstly his love for his son Simon (who sadly passed away in October 2013 and was a great and passionate advocate for his Father's works.) and secondly his succinct reasons for writing.

TO JULIAN SIMON FIELD BURRAGE
who at the moment of writing will
soon achieve the great age of four.
From somebody who loves him.

In War is War I admitted being a professional writer, or in other words one who depends for his bread and cheese and beer on writing, typing or dictating strings of sentences which his masters, the Public, are kind enough to buy and presumably to read.

The book brought me letters from a few old friends and a great many new ones. A large percentage of the new friends, who missed having seen that my identity was rather unkindly betrayed by the Press, wrote and asked (a) who I was and (b) what sort of stories did I write?

The answer to the second question will be found in the following pages. The answer to the first question is 'Nobody Much', worse luck.

Most of these stories were written with the intention of giving the reader a pleasant shudder, in the hope that he will take a lighted candle to bed with him—for candle-makers must be considered in these hard times. Some have already made their bow from the pages of the monthly magazines. The best have, quite naturally, been rejected.